TODAY
I LEARNED
IT WAS YOU

TODAY
I LEARNED
IT WAS YOU

EDWARD
RICHE

ANANSI

Published in Canada in 2016 by House of Anansi Press Inc.
www.houseofanansi.com

20 19 18 17 16   1 2 3 4 5

Library and Archives Canada Cataloguing in Publication

Riche, Edward, author
Today I learned it was you / Edward Riche.

Issued in print and electronic formats.
ISBN 978-1-4870-0057-8 (paperback).—ISBN 978-1-4870-0058-5 (html)

I. Title.

PS8585.I198T63 2016   C813'.54   C2015-907621-8
C2015-907622-6

Book design: Alysia Shewchuk
Cover image: © moopsi / Shutterstock

We acknowledge for their financial support of our publishing program
the Canada Council for the Arts, the Ontario Arts Council, and the Government of Canada
through the Canada Book Fund.

Printed and bound in Canada

MIX
Paper from
responsible sources
FSC® C004071

For Frances

TODAY
I LEARNED
IT WAS YOU

HARRY RECALLED THE white spire, a dog's tooth, and walls scalloped so they caught every which way of the light; a blue-bellied, tide-borne cathedral of ice.

He was in Newfoundland in the role of Doctor Bradman, for the final performances of an unfortunate touring production of *Blithe Spirit*. It was 1979 and then, as now, early June. Fog like mortar closed the airport at Torbay and three nights in St. John's, Newfoundland, became four and then five.

There was a delicious dereliction about the town in the day. Even as the lilac- and canary-coloured clapboard was coming down round their ears, the local players were putting on shows. Song was a reflex.

Their ceaseless talk was in a mongrel accent, Elizabethan doused with fishy Irish.

None of them had a dime.

At dawn Harry had quit an itinerant party continuing aboard the Portuguese fishing trawler *Jose Caçào*. Down the

1

gangplank, stepping tenderly along the apron, making for his bed in the Hotel Newfoundland, he saw that the great bank of mist had retreated in the night to unveil, at the harbour narrows, an iceberg as high as the hills. An iceberg! Of course Harry stayed on.

The natives didn't realize it, but their isolation and logy progress meant the culture was a vestige of an inshore fishery from the seventeenth and eighteenth centuries. Harry didn't realize it, but outside the tight circle of "rubber boot radicals," with whom he fast fell in, the desire to assimilate with modern, mainland Canada was general.

The locals loved easily. Harry'd never been as happy as he was with young, sweet-as-candy, ever-high Phillip. Later, with stolid Tony, "My Bayman Tony," there wasn't bliss but there was contentment.

Harry Davenant stayed on. Lived alone now; apartment with a rooster silhouette, a Gaulish cock, stencilled into the linoleum floor of what must have been the dining room before the building was divided, horsehair plaster walls painted with lead gloss, insulated with paperbacks, back of a house on Cochrane Street that listed toward the water.

Harry was now approaching his Lear years, getting older and no wiser, with change feeling strange and in reduced circumstances. But he was childless. You'd want the trials and joys of daughters to truly know Lear.

It was never going to happen.

There was less interest in stories in St. John's these days. Mining was the rage. When the theatre closed and he'd gone in search of other work, there were positions in the extraction of ores and tars from the earth, but he was in possession of none of the requisite skills. At his age Harry imagined finding a job doing something like reshelving books in a library or helping out at a museum or archive, but they told him such occupations no longer existed and he must take a job serving coffee and donuts or, as it came to be after a perfunctory interview, as a security guard.

Lloyd Purcell, heartless film and telly prick that he was, taunted Harry with "RADA to nada in forty," but Harry resolved he was going to make the best of it. He was eager to drive a car again. (He'd been so long without a valid driver's licence he'd been obliged to take a written test.) His rounds took him to quarters of the boom town he'd still, after these thirty-five odd years, never seen. The early summer was unusually clement and Harry was out and about instead of behind a desk in the basement of the LSPU Hall Theatre. He was moving and in the daylight.

Harry turned the company car, a black Impala, in a lax loop round the parking lot of an unnamed strip mall in the west end. This was the city's boundary when he'd first arrived; now there was more population beyond it than before.

The fluorescent lights seemed to have been mistakenly left on at Elite Dry Cleaning and there was no sign of life within. The offices of Atlantech Petroleum Services next door were dark. Chafe's Suprette was shuttered. Harry's supervisor said the convenience store had been held up so many times the operators threw in the towel.

Harry picked up the clipboard from the passenger seat to record that at 19:14 15/06/2013 all was in order when he noticed, at the westernmost side of the building, a cheap compact car, unmanned, its driver's-side door open. He did not know enough to identify the vehicle's make. He was going to have to work on that, get a picture book or something.

How to play it? Harry parked the Impala and got out.

He was in livery, black windbreaker with "SECURITY" across the back. The Sentry crest on his ball cap looked official, almost martial at a distance, but verged to costume on closer inspection, a theatrical rather than cinematic piece. A long and heavy Maglite worked as a prop cudgel.

His notion to let the flashlight swing was convincing. Though his last eleven years had been spent in theatre administration, he was still in possession of his craft. Rounding the corner of the building, heading for the alley behind, he was in control of his breathing and gait, keeping time, trying on a soldier's swagger. He rationalized that the paunch stretching his coat lent him substance.

He would routinely vomit before going on stage and he felt queasy now.

There was a man back there, holding open or caught closing his trousers. Seeing Harry, the man ducked behind a dumpster.

"Excuse me, sir," said Harry. Deference was all wrong, he thought. He walked on, recalling hard men in Hackney pubs. "Oi! Get here."

The undernourished, middle-aged fellow buttoned his tan cords. He was wearing a hoodie with the logo of a local hockey team, the St. John's "IceCaps."

"Just taking a leak," he lied.

"Piss at the Dairy Queen," said Harry, still moving forward

and gratified to see the man shuffling in retreat.

"Didn't want to buy anything so . . ."

"Next time treat yourself to a Blizzard. Move on."

"Yes, sir. Sorry." The man seemed to be considering whether he should go all the way around the building to get back to his car but finally scurried, eyes averted, past Harry.

Six days on the job and this was his first confrontation. Hearing the door of the unidentified car slam and its tires crackling over degenerating pavement, Harry thought Security Guard was a role he could play in a long run.

At Harry's feet were the foamy filters from cigarettes, irregular beads of glass—emerald and amber—and a plastic comb. Further along was a discarded fleshy-pink condom elementally related to the bits of chewing gum stomped into the ground around it. The plastic lids of take-away coffees were as fallen leaves. The backstage of enterprise. The storefronts tried to say "All is well, you are prosperous, we have what you need to go forward." It was a performance too. Ladies and gentlemen, please take your seats, thought Harry, the show is always about to begin.

Next stop was Bowring Park. Lovely that, he thought.

Harry had grown despondent as the funding for the theatre was trimmed and again trimmed, the budget eventually cut to a point where the place could no longer operate. But he was beginning to see that his time labouring there was a sentence as much as a sinecure. Fortune was kinder than it first seemed. As long as he put in these late shifts, he made more money as a security guard than he ever had as an artistic director. It was funny really. But Chekov-funny, sad-funny.

He steered from the parking lot into traffic and headed south, noticing that his hands were unsteady.

Near the park entrance Harry pulled the Impala over and turned off the engine. Families and couples and dog-walkers were taking their time leaving via the front gate. The stone bridge and the pavement were dappled as the sun descended behind an irregular ridge of horse chestnuts and copper beeches.

He craved a smoke like he hadn't in years. A straight job was marked by punching in and out with stipulated breaks. Running the theatre, directing shows, was unremitting anxiety. When he would awaken in the night, the worries of his harried day invariably rushed in. No longer. He'd given too much of himself and with scant thanks in the end. For whom had he even quit smoking? It was for his bayman Tony, and Tony was gone.

A young family passed. Three small children were being herded to a car, the father and mother sniping at one another, she with a hand up to deflect and mute his complaints. Merely unhappy in their own way? No, there was more, there was flight in their stride. Harry stepped out of his vehicle and put on his cap.

"Is everything all right?"

The father spoke. "You with security?"

"Sentry."

"You'd better go down there. Fucking skeets drinking in the park."

"Language, Jesus, Brian," said the mother, buckling her children into the back seat of a sedan Harry did know to be a Volkswagen of some sort.

"Not like they didn't hear worse today," said the father to
Harry.

"I'll see to it," said Harry, thinking the model of car might
be an Altima.

"You should...maybe you should call...the police," said
the father.

"Let me check it out. Thank you for bringing it to my
attention."

A band of maroon low in the sky reminded Harry to carry
his hefty flashlight.

IMMEDIATELY AFTER THE gate, the Waterford River was diverted
to make an ornamental pond for swans and too many ducks.
There was something amiss with the large milk-coloured bird
sailing closest to him; a wing was trailing in the water and
the animal was preening its breast with annoyance. Harry
needed a closer look but could not think how one beckoned
such a creature. And were not swans notoriously peevish
birds? Want to give you a nip. He would mention it to park
staff when he saw them.

There was solvent on the air, nail polish? Harry turned
and looked up. Paint, aerosol: a hot blot of chromium yellow
sprayed on the crotch of Peter Pan was trickling stickily, drying
heavier than honey, molten and metallic.

The ageless boy was in bronze, atop a plinth featuring
woodland creatures—rabbits and squirrels—in relief. There
was a fairy, caped in translucent wings, who might have been
Tinkerbell.

Harry knew the statue's London double. Kensington

Garden. He recalled his hand in his mother's: "Peter!"

Harry could not see or hear the vandals, so set off for a bridge under which, he recalled from a briefing, teenage louts took cover.

Almost halfway there, Harry nosed a ribbon of marijuana smoke coming through a hedge of rhododendron, its red blooms losing their colour in the dusk. Trailing the scent, six paces on he found a pathway, tricked out with uneven stones, that he knew led to a memorial for soldiers lost in the Great War.

The hooligans had congregated in a hollow defined by a wall of remembrance and a rise crowned by another bronze, that of a buck caribou. This statue was of a series, the other monuments in France and Belgium — at Beaumont Hamel, Gueudecourt, Masnières, Monchy-le-Preux, and Kortrijk — where the best of a generation of Newfoundlanders died for the King of England.

They were in and out of shadow, seven eight nine of them. There was a tall one with a bluish-complexion that must have been Sudanese. Two girls both in stretchy summer tops; one wore a tiny skirt, the other pyjama bottoms patterned with death-heads and, he noticed, orange plastic dollar-store flip-flops. Rest of them were the sort of pasty-faced corner boys whose role it was to make what trouble they couldn't find in St. John's.

"The Lost B'ys." All these years and Harry still couldn't do the accent.

An emptied spray-paint can bounced across the cobble, the plastic pea within making a sound like a baby's rattle.

"Mall cop," one of them said.

The pack was shifting, whether to surround him or flee Harry could not tell.

"Clear out, *Skipper.*" A boy-a man-an ape, sixteen or seventeen years, pushed off his perch on the ground at the metal caribou's front hooves to drop and land in front of Harry.

The ruffian's T-shirt was sizes too big and billowed, but his arms were like hawsers taut from the pull of a ship. He had a wide mouth and raven hair.

"Go now," said Harry. "Leave the park. That'll give you a lead on the police."

"Fuck off." The boy blew the words into Harry's face, into his mouth.

How did it go? *"Met so near with their lips that their breaths embraced"*? Harry's one and only Iago, the Citizens Theatre in Glasgow, never really pulling it off. If he had his time back . . .

A missile of some sort, a stone he supposed, hit Harry behind his right ear, drawing wet. He turned in the direction from which it was launched and saw the tag on the wall. More spray paint, in a nonsensical bulbous script. The same sick-making yellow pigment defiling the names of the brave, a streak of bile offending the memory marked there of Mr. Edgecombe and Mr. Porter and Mr. Richardson.

"How dare you?" Harry said softly. They cackled. Someone spit.

He spun around, putting his flashlight-baton in the widest arc. The black-haired boy was quick but Harry caught his hand, shattering the glass eye of the lantern on something bony. The boy howled.

A pole, a branch maybe, bounced off Harry's windpipe.

A force came in from behind, powerful enough to feel like it was passing through him laying track. A heel on his spine sent Harry face forward.

He heard their leader again, yelping and yipping.

Blast. Tremor. Rupture.

ONE

THE TEMPTATION ALWAYS existed, now that tablets had replaced
paper files, to go online and surf the Web during the Monday
city council meetings. Matt Olford knew that the high back of
the mayor's chair precluded anyone in the gallery from seeing
what it was he was reading. The city councillors of St. John's
bellied up to a large horseshoe-shaped table facing him and saw
only that he was looking at his screen. With Councillor Wally
O'Neill on his feet, Matt succumbed and found Puck Daddy
under his "favorites." Matt now enjoyed reading about hockey
more than watching it. There seemed to be twice as many
games as necessary played by men twice as big and thrice as
fast on a surface half its former size. Accounts he read ran in
his head at the easier pace he'd played the game.

Matt saw that Ron Hextall was denying yet another rumour
that he was going to leave Philly and his post as general manager of the Flyers. Matt always read the stories about Hextall.
The big goalkeeper had come close to single-handedly defeating

11

the Edmonton Oilers in the 1987 Stanley Cup final and denying
Matt his providential championship ring. They gave Hextall,
the goalie on the losing side, the Conn Smythe Trophy for most
valuable player that year. Hextall earned it losing to a squad
led by the best to ever play the game. Won it in losing. Was
that somehow, with the passage of time, a greater achievement
than victory itself?

"...swam in it, fished in it, drank it..." Wally was address-
ing a report critical of the water quality of a stream in his ward.

Matt had taken two half-assed shots on Hextall in the series, both easily kicked away. Hextall surrounded himself with
a force field of will and Matt couldn't get near enough to pose
a threat. Matt was on the fourth line, up from the AHL farm
team in Halifax to replace an injured player, and was given
little ice time, a fact for which he was then secretly grateful.

"...everything runs downhill sure, and ya knows what dat
means..."

Matt deserved the ring. They called on him five times in
that series to take critical faceoffs. Five-for-five, one an assist.
Five-for-five in the finals. That was something. He answered
the call and that made him champion. And certainly mayor of
St. John's, Newfoundland. He deserved the ring.

"...stuff didn't come from outer space, did it? Everything, if
you looks at it, is 'natural,' comes from here, a different mixture
das all. Oil is natural, comes out of the ground. Metals might
be heavy but if we dug 'em up dey must be organic, right? Sure
what are PCPs but—?"

"PCBs Councillor O'Neill. PCP is the drug, I think," Matt
said so that it appeared he'd been paying attention.

"Wha?" said Wally.

"PCP is the drug," said Ward 2 councillor Cy Jardine, "Horse trank."

"Wha?" said Wally again.

"The toxin we are concerned with, present in Grates Brook, is PCB, polychlorinated biphenyl." Councillor Alessandra Cappello stood to speak. "You're confusing it with PCP, the street drug. I'm not certain what the letters in PCP stand for. I think they used to call it Angel Dust."

Alessandra Cappello did not belong in the company of these buffoons, but Matt was grateful for her presence. Matt felt Councillor Cappello did not fully understand, or, in her difficult European leftie way, chose not to understand how the market economy worked, how development was an engine that kept the city moving, how money was a fuel and a lubricant. But on most other civic matters she and he agreed. She raised the level of debate in the chamber. Matt liked to hear her voice. Perhaps the faintest trace of an Italian accent remained (she spoke better English than anyone on council), the music of her mother tongue coloured her speech and she occasionally let a word or phrase drop in, but mostly it was the tone. He wished, when she spoke, she might never stop. But she did and Wally started up again.

"Maybe dat's what's happening to me, all dat Angel Dust in da water."

"That must be it, Wally, all the horse trank that's after getting into your system," said Councillor Jardine. "Or, what's the new one, bath salts?"

Bluff and ruddy Cyril Jardine, the councillor seated nearest

Matt's left, was always good for a laugh, thought Matt, for poking fun, but good for nothing more. (The deputy mayor, Councillor Wendy Kennedy, sat nearest his right hand and was, befitting their comparative placement, the antithesis of Jardine in temperament; dour, humourless, all business.)

"Bat' salts? Dat da one made da fella in Florida eat da face off buddy?" Wally affirmed before returning to the agenda. "All I knows is dat if you ask the crowd dat live up to what used to be called da Gullies, or any of dem dat got a place down on da lower road if dey would rather have a job making paint or . . ."

Did Wally cultivate that "t'ick" accent? Matt thought it might be heavier in these evening public meetings than it was in the private meetings they held in the afternoon. He said "nickelll" and "milllk" and "fillum" like someone from St. John's, but otherwise spoke like a proper bayman. You dropped your *h*'s in 'olyrood and picked them up in *H*avondale but there was no locus to Wally's lilt. And wasn't Wally from the Southern Shore, or those parts of the Southern Shore now subsumed by the expansion of the city? Some fishing village recently exurbed? Maybe that explained the townie taint on his tongue. Maybe it was his mother's Conche. The only person on council who had any trouble with it was Ms. Cappello, and Matt wondered if Wally sometimes didn't lean on it to antagonize her.

Matt checked his emails. From his brother, Len: probably a GIF of some tool messing themselves up, the looped falling off a ladder, or crashing a mountain bike, something head-splitting or nut-crushing that was supposed to be funny that Matt didn't get. His Camry was due for servicing. Six invites to events that he would forward to his secretary, Audrey Manning, without opening. He only bothered to read the email from his daughter, Katie, who was majoring in Montreal at McGill.

"I'm assuming you put that $2000 in my bank account. Thanks. Wasn't hinting but thanks. Mom is now bombing me with Christian stuff a couple times a day. Weird to me. Anyway thanks Luv U Dad."

His wife, Patty, the daughter of lapsed Catholics, announced six months ago that she had joined the Christian and Missionary Alliance, an evangelical Protestant church. Their kids, Katie and Jack, who were now in regular receipt of religious literature from their mother, kept asking their father how and why this happened. Matt didn't have an answer. Were they still talking about waste water?

"...everyone needs a drop of paint and we know how useless the environmentally friendly stuff was on the roads last winter..."

Jesus, they were.

TWO

IT WAS EVERYTHING Alessandra Cappello could do to stop herself from doodling like a teenage girl in the back of class. In a forty-year-old woman it was an unfortunate tic. *Withdrawing*, luscious English word. Her fellow St. John's city councillor Wally O'Neill was driving her into herself. It wasn't merely Wally's ignorance; it was that he wore it as a badge of honour. He laughed at his own errors in the accurate calculation that it helped voters identify with him. Wally could even join in with those sniggering at what he'd said, echo the fits and giggles when he was unintentionally funny, could laugh with them as they laughed at him. This was his fourth term in office. He may as well have re-election posters saying "We All Make Mistakes—Vote Wally O'Neill."

This was Alessandra's first term in office. She would not run again. She would use her husband Jules's failing health as an excuse, knowing everyone would accept it and in doing so feel entitled to observe, behind her back, that it was the price

17

she paid for marrying a man so many years her senior.

"...T'anks, your Worship..."

Had Mayor Olford taken mercy and cut Wally off? The mayor could do that sort of thing without offending. It was a skill. Alessandra thought Matt Olford was wilfully naive about the dangers of the unchecked expansion of the city. He bought into some neo-liberal myths about what was proving to be the trickle-up economics of late capitalism. But on every other account she thought him an almost perfect fit for the job.

"...one udder matter..."

Stronzo. More from that donkey.

Alessandra had assumed she could not win the seat in the municipal election. Her run was an opportunity to draw attention to issues concerning the preservation of some older neighbour-hood features being lost in a recent flurry of urban development. It was a break from her job at the university's map library.

The campaign was during a clear-aired August and September. She enjoyed walking around canvassing, talking up her concerns, offering solutions, meeting people. Nobody was as surprised as she with her narrow victory. It was her secret that St. John's liked her more than she did it.

On went Wally.

"...is an ideal location for the Newfoundland and Labrador Sports Hall of Fame..."

Where was an ideal location? For what? She thought they were discussing the cleanup of the former paint factory site. Alessandra should have been listening more closely.

"This is kind of out of the blue, Councillor O'Neill," said the mayor.

"They are bursting out of their current digs, Your Worship,"
said Wally.

"Is no one interested in running it as a theatre?" asked
Councillor Dunn.

"You're proposing turning the LSPU Hall, the theatre, into
the Sports Hall of Fame?" asked Alessandra. No one answered.
Alessandra signalled to the mayor that she wished to speak.

"We are definitely not getting into show business," said
the mayor, indicating with a glance that he'd seen Alessandra,
"but..."

"That theatre wasn't much of a business, 'show' or otherwise," said Wally.

"Who has the floor? I believe Councillor Cappello," said
the mayor. "Can we please..."

"You must be in the Sports Hall of Fame, Your Worship,"
offered Councillor Neary.

"Hall of Shame maybe, Councillor Neary," answered the
mayor.

"Matt Olford will be in the Hall of Fame, there is no doubt
about that," said Wally.

"Someone will have to shoot me before I can be stuffed and
mounted, Councillor. Can we please have order. Councillor
Cappello has the floor."

"Thank you, Mayor Olford." Alessandra stood. "There
was never a formal arrangement with the LSPU Hall Theatre
because we assumed responsibility on such short notice, in an
emergency, really. They hadn't anticipated losing their funding.
The bank would have taken the building if we hadn't stepped
in. No one ever said at the time that the city was going to

operate it. There was an assumption, mistaken, it seems, that some group from the arts community would come forward with a plan. There have been a few requests to rent it but there are liability issues that would have to be worked out if we were to oblige. That said, I think the understanding has always been that it would continue, in some fashion, to be a theatre."

"Councillor O'Neill." Mayor Olford acknowledged Wally. Alessandra sat.

"I think the Sports Hall of Fame would do a great job of preserving the old building," Wally said. Alessandra stood again.

"That it's a heritage structure isn't the only issue; it's having a downtown theatre." Alessandra sat. Wally stood.

"I knows, I knows. We have to wait. Knows it. But . . . just saying *but . . . if . . .* the theatre thing doesn't pan out, even with the limited parking it would be a grand spot for the Sports Hall of Fame. I has a sense dat people aren't going to the theatre so much anymore what wit Netflix and games on dere phones, but dat's a guess. If people wants to go to shows down dere den I can see it. But if not we can't keep it open just to say it is."

"It was," observed Councillor Mercer, "the Longshoreman's Protective Union — LSPU — Hall before it was ever a theatre. Longshoremen went the way of the dodo when shipping containers came along. Maybe theatre is a thing of the past. Maybe smartphones are theatre's shipping containers . . . I dunno . . . but things change."

"Dare I send this to committee?" asked the mayor. There was a desultory murmur of agreement that such should be done. "Any new business?"

Neary stood.

"We may have some people living in Bowring Park," he said.

"Living?" said the mayor.

"Camping? I dunno, like a tramp or tramps. Homeless. Are you allowed to call people gypsies, anymore?"

"Can't call someone retarded anymore," said Wally.

"Roma," said Councillor Cappello. No one gave a sign of having heard her.

"It's 'gyped' you can't say," said Councillor Mercer.

"And you wants to be queer before you calls anyt'ing gay," said Wally. "D'know dat?"

"There are reports," Councillor Neary continued, "of people living in the wooded area out there."

"That's probably the same crowd who vandalized the war memorial," said Wally, putting his fist to the table. "Sleveens who were at Peter Pan's no-no place."

"That was on Peter's privates?" asked Jardine.

"Yes b'y," said Wally, "right up under his dress. Sick wha'?"

"Tunic," said Deputy Mayor Kennedy. "It's a tunic."

"What about security? Why haven't...?" the mayor queried.

"Sentry has been having a devil of a time keeping staff. Price of the boom, Your Worship. Good workers are made a better offer and move on. People from the company were genuinely sorry and are on it."

"You know that 'on it' means 'we haven't yet done it,'" said the mayor, earning a few chuckles. "It's a corollary of 'it is what it is,' which means, 'it's something I won't do anything about.'" He pointed to Alessandra. "And please don't say 'I told you so,' Councillor Cappello."

Alessandra had been alone on council in opposing the contracting out of security at city parks.

"The Parks and Public Spaces committee meets Wednesday," said Alessandra. "If we can have an update then?" She looked to the table at which a trio of city staff sat and got three nods.

THREE

WHAT'S THE WORD?

The thing the thing the knife the blade thing for . . . for the face, for shaving, that simple thing?

Name of the thing, the thing with the . . . the . . . maw, the clamp for the . . . name of the thing?

He stirred the contents of a drawer full of unctions and ointments with his hand. Italian face cream. "Nailclippers" he knew.

Where was he last? He flew out of Milan. Fish every day in Genoa. Potatoes.

No, no these were a woman's things in the drawer and he was looking for . . .

If he had one in his hand he would know what it was called. If there was a package he'd read it.

The bloody thing, yes bloody . . . you'd cut yourself your whiskers.

The thing was . . . he knew its its its haecceity, its quality of being the thing it was, its thisness. Or was that because he was thinking of it from without? Was it its thatness, its quiddity?

Thisness thatness

This is

The is

This is the thesis

This is

Went to a lecture by Sir Bernard Williams once. That was Oxford.

Where were we?

Had he pissed? Washed his hands? He could smell the soap, lavender like Aix. Jays screaming outside. Summer. Leaves on the trees. Then why was he going to class? No. He was home. It was summer. This was St. John's. He was in Newfoundland. He was looking for the thing. Name of:

He knew what it was, its qualities, only the name escaped him. Got away from him.

He was going to talk to a doctor about this. Consult a physician. Confusion, the confusion was the issue more than the memory. He could remember everything even the kettle and he knew that Corte-Real's caravel was the

It went out of his mind.

What was he doing up here? Why had he come? He decided to go back downstairs.

And fear. Afraid in his heart, a bird cupped in your hands. Jules was going to make an appointment with his doctor and demand something for the dread. He was a man and he could not be afraid of things. There were ways of coping with every other symptom, you could write yourself notes, you could.

There was something else too, he was going to talk to, who was it? About what?

Someone was coming into the house. He couldn't remember there being a door over there. Was it a window one time and they'd renovated? They were coming right in. It was a woman, coming right in like that. Should he hide? No, she'd seen him. Was she the cleaner? No, he knew her, she was a grad. Student. Wasn't she?

FOUR

ALESSANDRA MORE AND more often found Jules like this, adrift. He was standing in a spot in the kitchen where one didn't stand, in reach of nothing, on no heading. There was a mien of terror on his face when first she entered. It was replaced by an attempt at a smile.

"Were you getting something to eat, Jules?"

"No. No. I'm not hungry."

"You haven't shaved? Did you shower? You have a doctor's appointment early tomorrow morning, remember? First appointment so we won't have to wait."

"The doctor I did remember. I will go back up now and get a shower." Jules lit up. "Shave with a *razor. Non fate tardi.*" He headed upstairs.

"Late for what? The doctor is tomorrow," asked Alessandra, but Jules was gone.

How little medical science could do for Jules. Surely, Alessandra thought, with legions of baby boomers about to be so afflicted, Big Pharma would concoct something that alleviated the symptoms. Surely there was money in that? Not necessarily anything for the aphasia that had Jules slipping into Italian, or the forgetfulness, but certainly a balm against the anxiety, the panic that seemed to more frequently seize him.

Jules's Italian was sound but sterile when Alessandra met him. His was the fluency of an exceptional student, learned in classes and libraries, not in taverns, not at Dalla Marisa. He wanted to study Venetian dialect but it wasn't often formally taught, so that part of the archival work, the local diplomacy and barter with the librarians and archivists, fell to Alessandra. The Cappellos were a "new" family of Venice, only in Veneta since the fourteenth century. They'd been doges and procurates of St. Mark's and traders. Venetian she knew.

Her father, Piero, clung to the status of being a Cappello in La Dominante even as the palazzo, its piles rotting, sank in the mud. He tried not liking Jules and opposing the marriage. But Jules was dashing then and engaging and the two men got on. Jules suffered Piero's tiresome *Indipendenza Veneta* arguments and his cockamamie economic theories without complaint or correction.

Jules's subject, the mariner and mountebank Zuan Cabotto, one of the many reputed discoverers of Newfoundland, fled Venice owing money to a Cappello, and Piero joked that he would hold Jules to the debt. Though Jules was a lowly scholar there was some family money, and his attentions let Piero forget the Cappellos were in hock, that the lagoon was reclaiming the city, and that Italy was a shambles. Alessandra's mother, Marina, confessed she loved Jules more than her daughter loved him but refused to bless the union. Jules, Marina told Alessandra, was too old for her and the marriage would come to grief; a judgement proven fair when, not many years later, her new friends in St. John's started having babies and Alessandra did the math.

She and Jules moved to a mythical Canada; a liberal social democracy, the fancy, she later realized, of a generation of bright postgraduates, drunk from travel to (but never quotidian life in) Scandinavia and France, a fiction forced on a bunch of frontier hicks who had more recently organized, taken back their country, and then sold it cheap to resource multinationals. There was a deep, core anti-intellectualism about the place, a trait of which Jules always knew but neglected to ever mention, a lie of omission that Alessandra was beginning to feel was a betrayal. The country wasn't Norway; it was northernmost North Dakota. The political left (to which Alessandra inclined) in Canada was a loose assembly of self-righteous touts for self-evident causes, sharing only their terror of the central economic tenets of socialism. They were more like retired teachers in a church group than agents of political change.

But in the colonial outpost of Newfoundland, where Ontario-born Jules accepted a full professorship, there was no ideology whatsoever. It was tribal here.

There was no one with whom she could share these thoughts. She was a foreigner, so not entitled to grouse.

Alessandra looked out the kitchen window and on to the yard. It was early June and an uncommonly balmy one so far. The leaves still wore a newborn sheen and pallor. The tulips were only now in full bloom. Until recently she had not missed

Venice. Not missed the tidal funk and the unending staying of the sinking, not missed the garish tourism, not missed the contradiction of constant complaint and resignation that had become the national norm.

But this spring she dreamed of wisteria and soupy risotto with *sciopeti*, with shrimp and asparagus and *nero di seppia* and a heat the sun never brought to Newfoundland.

Even to return for a restorative visit.

But Jules was going nowhere. He was her tether.

She listened but did not hear the shower running. He'd forgotten.

FIVE

MATT'S SECRETARY, AUDREY Manning, knew which events
Mayor Olford wished to skip and which he would attend.
Petitions were continual; Celebrity Karaoke in Support of
Cystic Fibrosis hosted by the Kinsmen of Mount Pearl. Avalon
HAM Radio. Kiwanis Music Festival. St. John's Clean and
Beautiful. Monarchist. Horticulturist. New Canadians. Old
Newfoundlanders. Blind. Deaf. Lame. Halt. Riddled. There
wasn't an amateur sports association that did not request his
presence at their fund raisers—from Under 16 Girls Bowling
to Masters Slo-Pitch, they all called. To avoid offending any
of the many groups involved in minor hockey by favouring
one or the other, he begged off all of them. Matt was obliged
to lace up every year and play a charity match for the Brain
Injury Association: local politicians versus media (he'd dressed
for the journalists last contest, as their numbers were in such
decline they couldn't ice a full team). He always dreaded the
game, always contemplated bowing out but always ended up

31

enjoying himself, always scored a couple of easy goals for a
laugh. He did a couple of tennis things because his daughter,
Katie, was involved when she was younger. Matt took other
sports as they came. With the rising costs and concussions of
hockey, soccer was now as popular.

"Don't forget you have Kids Eat Smart tonight," said Audrey.
Matt nodded. Making sure kids got a nutritious lunch and even
breakfast at school; this was one he wanted to support.

"Right. Is that...?" he asked.

"Yep, dinner."

"It would be. That hotel food...you know...it kills me."

"It's not good?"

"It's...I dunno. Hate hotels," said Matt.

"And I have to confirm you at the Board of Trade luncheon
next week."

"That's?"

"Imogene Hume," said Audrey. "Wrote some book about
music."

"Yes, right, I told someone I would go...so, yes, confirm."
Music seemed an odd choice for the Board of Trade, but a welcome change from the usual market shill. Matt's late mother
was a music teacher at an elementary school. She owned a
collection of classical stuff on Deutsche Grammophon vinyl
that, filed, was at least two metres wide. In a house that was
never as strict as those of his friends, one of the few prohibitions
was on Matt touching the treasured discs. Those records—
one night Chopin, the next Bartók or Brahms—and a glass
of affordable wine were among his mother's few indulgences.
"That all, Audrey?"

"Don't forget Parks and Public Spaces Committee Wednesday afternoon."

"It was mentioned in the council meeting. People living in Bowring Park apparently."

"And there is a man outside to see you." Audrey checked a sheet. "Clayton Ivy."

"About what?"

"Hockey cards."

CLAYTON IVY STOOD as Matt exited his office. "Mr. Olford."

"Mr. Ivy." Matt took the hand offered. "What do you have?"

Ivy off-gassed tars and nicotine, like his car was his toxic terrarium. He fished in the front pouch of his St. John's Ice Caps hoodie and withdrew three hockey cards, each in a sized plastic sleeve.

"Three cards. I was hoping you could sign them. If it's not a problem?"

"Not at all," said Matt. Though it was. Young people were one thing, but adult collectors of memorabilia gave him the creeps. And did not three cards mean the thin man meant to trade them? "Do you have a pen or marker...?" A fine-point Sharpie was proffered.

"There's two from your Stanley Cup season and the third is from 91–92," said Ivy, handing Matt the card from Matt's final season in the NHL. This card featured the picture Matt favoured, caught taking a sharp turn on the ice, skates throwing snow, his attention on a puck out of frame like an animal hunting, a predator detecting a stirring in the grass. He signed his name to the front and turned the card over. This was Matt then,

Matthew Olford
Center/Centre

Height: 6'1" **Weight:** 202 **Shoots:** L

Born: 6-3-61, St. John's, Nfld

Home: Toronto, Ont

Last Amateur Club:
Trois-Rivières Draveurs 1984–85

Acquired: 4th Round Draft Pick, 1981

NHL RECORD/FICHE DANS LA LNH

Year	Team	GP	G	A	Pts	PIM
86–87	Oilers	11	1	4	5	2
87–88	Oilers	69	4	33	37	24
88–89	Oilers	46	1	12	13	20
89–90	Nordiques	60	4	20	24	14
90–91	Nordiques	19	1	9	10	10
91–92	Senators	11	1	3	4	0

"The Stanley Cup Year cards are more valuable. Obviously," said Ivy.

"Sure," said Matt, signing the cards from his stint on the triumphant Oilers. "Like what?"

"In pristine condition like this, twenty-five bucks maybe."

"Sorry? Twenty-five bucks?"

"I'll trade the duplicate. Less for the later card, first season for the Sens but..."

"Got it."

"How was that team?"

"The Senators? It was all right. I was having some injury problems. My hand."

"You got my vote. For mayor."

"Thanks for that."

Ivy slipped the cards back into their plastic sleeves.

SIX

LLOYD PURCELL KNEW that his brother, Dave, had rushed to secure his tiny wine cellar before flying off to "blow eighty-five days in the middle of France." The metal of the bolt was shiny and there was a litter of coiled wood shavings and sawdust on the floor below. Dave, wisely, did not trust his big brother with the stash beneath the stairs. Lloyd wondered if Dave had purposely left the signs that the lock was recently installed where they could be seen. A wine cellar seemed awfully grand for a house in Rabbittown.

Lloyd thirsted, but it was too early to start in on the Irish. A glass of red was the ticket.

Perhaps he should have gone to rehab in Los Angeles, back when he could afford it. What sort of discount regional facilities existed in Newfoundland, he wondered. Doubtlessly dreary joints jammed up with skanky court-mandated clients. And he was sure to know half of the people in there, would have gone to school with them. "Jaysus Murphy, if it isn't Lloyd Purcell,

37

back from the States, must be in for 'the blow' are you?"

Yes, a glass of red to steel himself in advance of settling down to create a Facebook page in ... "support?" he supposed ... of Harry Davenant.

Social media — another of the stakes driven into Lloyd's career. Facebook was akin to walking around the house naked with the curtains thrown open, the village gawking at your dangling junk. There were only so many "eye hours" out there, and every one of them dedicated to computer screens and phones was bread taken from Lloyd's mouth. The movies were dying. The new twentysomething media moguls had figured out a way to make the audience pay for the privilege of providing their own scripts, and then further humiliate them by having them painstakingly type them out by thumb.

Shag it, he thought, time to tackle the ugly business. He opened the laptop sitting on Dave's dining room table.

It asked how he wished to proceed. No, he did not want to create a page for himself. He'd so far managed to navigate the professional writing life without one. And without a goddamn Twitter account. His agent, Mike Vargas, back in Los Angeles, kept hounding Lloyd to "get in the game," to start tweeting his every banal thought in an effort to promote himself. Wasn't the shill Mike's job? If that was now "the game," then Lloyd didn't wanna play.

When Lloyd crash-landed in Toronto, the crowd putting on his play at Theatre Passe Muraille wondered about "a social media strategy." They'd dropped the line of inquiry after Lloyd's unwelcome exposition on the futility of the echo chamber, how it was an orgy of self-congratulation, like-minds stroking each other. Lloyd's play was lauded by the critics, but no one went; not even the like-minded heard about it.

Lloyd scanned the computer screen. An "event"? It would be, he hoped. More a "spectacle" if all went according to plan. "Cause or Community." There it was: "Cause." Harry Davenant was going to be a "cause."

Facebook wanted his email. Lloyd was still using his AOL address from the States. A reminder that he was never allowed to return. Lloyd had burnt that bridge. Torched it, watched the scorched deck and trestle thunderously collapse into the river, hissing and gasping as it was dragged under by the torrent.

He searched his pockets for and found a cigarette, a Winston, another prompt to regret, an American brand for which he here paid a premium. And they only carried the foul things at a few shops in town. He purchased the fag he lit now, against Dave's strict prohibition against smoking in his house, at Caines Grocery and Confectionery on the east end of Duckworth Street, a place unchanged since Lloyd left St. John's all those years ago. For all the screen credits on pictures good and bad, and despite his above-the-line Hollywood friends, the fleeting tabloid television infamy of his drugs arrest had landed him back at Caines buying smokes. "Coke, a smoke, and a raisin square," they used to say; townie comfort food, stuff you could gum.

What a shithole St. John's was, he thought. How impossible to endure after having lived the life in Los Angeles. Thinking about it now it was simple; he missed only one thing, one thing in a profound way, in a way that made him ache . . . the sun. He missed the hot sun. Lloyd was born and raised on a slippery rock in the North Atlantic; the sun of Southern California breathed new, essential vitality into his shivering frame. There were a few stinking months during his stint in Toronto, immediately after his deportation, something like the warm air under the sheets of a sickbed, but nothing like Southern California heat, desert heat Baja heat Santa Anna heat.

He needed something to drink, so let it be Irish.

"Post a picture?" Facebook asked. Bambi? Or maybe that Richter painting of the tender young stag hidden in the saplings. No, play it straight, the straighter the better, the character's truth. "Acting" had spoiled so many of the best lines he'd crafted. You could never lose playing it straight. Maybe a copse of trees, suggesting Harry hiding within?

A bottle of Bushmills was next to the kitchen sink, in which was scuttled Lloyd's plate from breakfast. A clot of egg floated on water slicked with oil from a kipper. A window above looked out on an insignificant yard.

He shouldn't have strong drink so early in the day. Did he have to meet anyone later? He had Natalie Sommerville tomorrow; if the moment presented itself, he was considering asking her if he might borrow a few dollars. He had no other appointments. He would not connect with another living soul today.

The backyard supported little flora. There was a skeleton of kindling that must have once aspired to be a flowering shrub. And, he'd never noticed it before, there was an old wheelchair out there. That's what it was, an antique cart from a sanatorium, from a fever hospital, with Japanese knotweed, "Mile-a-Minute," they called it here, growing up through the spokes.

A wheelchair! That settled it; he poured a double dose into an unwashed glass.

SEVEN

PEOPLE SEARCHED, IN desperation, for meaning, searched the same way they clawed at garbage dumped on the kitchen floor for a lost wedding ring, Patty thought. Yet the answers were all around them. The traffic light, the mind to make road networks and cars and how we all knew and obeyed the rules, the illuminated softball pitch beyond the trees. It was, all of it, wondrous, and if you let yourself see it, see God's work, you could be always at peace.

What was the dark force that made people turn away from the bliss found in clarity and seek instead confusion? Pastor Maggs said it was Satan and Patty didn't think, from the way he talked about it, her minister was referring to some abstraction. Pastor Maggs was talking about an entity, about a being among us. This Patty could not see. Her muddle was of her own making; she'd done it to herself. Patty was confident she had never met the devil and was sure that Pastor Maggs was not suggesting that it was she.

Pastor Maggs's message was transparency; metaphors and symbols were confusion. What was wrong with embracing one simple, clear answer to all life's vexing questions? Why not accept the answer? The world could not have emerged from chaos; it absolutely, doubtlessly came from order.

She'd first heard Pastor Maggs's voice not in testament but in song. With her kids away in university, time opened like a vast plain in front of Patty, but these were dry and empty flats, a place to wander lost, not to breathe. She joined the Symphony Choir to fill some of the hours. She knew the pastor not as a man of faith but as a full-throated singer with perhaps more enthusiasm than tune, a belting tenor a couple of metres behind her left ear.

One day, during a break in a rehearsal for the *Messiah*, the woman in the chair next to Patty's, a woman about her own age named Melissa Cooper, broke down in tears. It turned out that Melissa had that morning put down her dog, a fifteen-year-old Jack Russell named Bette. Her tears were out of all proportion for the loss of an old dog, however beloved. Through the sobs, Patty heard and sympathized with Melissa's complaint; it wasn't the end of the dog but the end of another in a series of dogs that hit Melissa so hard. There was Bette and before her Valentine and before that Monk and when she was a girl they'd had Foster, a big Newfoundland, and Chilly a crackie they got from the pound that was the smartest dog there ever was. She was crying because there was one dog after another, there were the marriages, the births, the deaths, the graduations, the *Messiah* and all the rest and for what? And if another person told her to "get a new puppy straight away," Melissa swore she'd punch them. Pastor Maggs—Denis, he introduced himself as—was soon at Melissa's side. He told Melissa she was right to be sad about Bette, because mourning the dog's death was in fact the very essence of being alive. If a mere dog's life was meaningless, exactly how could it be felt so profoundly?

Patty thought the pastor kind and felt if she declined the invitation he extended after rehearsal to join his congregation, just one day, in worship, she would be ungrateful. So she went.

The traffic light changed and Patty continued driving east on Empire Avenue. The dandelions were in pissy riot on lawns untended by renters. Why should one flower be yellow and another red? Why would we have evolved to perceive the beauty in the things? Why did she miss her children so?

She saw a young man looking aged, face pained and peppered as if caught in a blast, fighting to climb a flat stretch of sidewalk. Drugs or mental illness, Patty supposed. If not God's work, whose?

EIGHT

BOTH BEDSIDE LAMPS were on. Patty lay on her side, her face turned so Matt could not tell if she was awake or asleep until she spoke.

"How was the Kids Eat Smart thing?" she asked.

"Long, otherwise not unpleasant."

"Food?"

"Not great. Chicken breast, you know."

"In a nice sauce or anything?" Patty turned on to her back to watch her husband undress.

"A gravy, I guess. I didn't pay much attention. Didn't eat much of it."

"Dessert?"

"I can't remember, didn't even taste it."

"You'd think, Kids Eat Smart, the food..."

"The cause and the thing are different." Matt stepped out of his trousers. The reliable yet never familiar current of hurt ran through his knee. And there was, of late, something hot in his hips.

"How was the council meeting?" Patty asked.

"Very Wally O'Neill." Matt climbed under the covers.

"If it weren't for you Wally would be mayor."

"No, I don't think so."

"He would."

"People aren't that stupid." Matt turned out his light. Patty followed his lead.

"They are sometimes."

"What did you eat, hon?" asked Matt.

"I made a grilled cheese and I had it with a glass of red wine and it was so delicious I can't tell you."

"Really." Matt laughed.

"Sometimes it's what you want. Simple things can be wonderful."

It felt good to close his eyes. Matt thought about the fundraising dinner and tried to recall to whom he'd spoken but did not possess the energy. It was an event like so many others. Good people working for such a good cause; he felt bad that he didn't have the will to remember what any of them said.

Wally O'Neill was stupid enough to be a danger, he thought. If Patty was right (it wasn't the first time she'd said that Wally wanted Matt's job) then Matt's otherwise uneventful mayoralty at least saved the city from getting Wally-ed. They needed more people like Alessandra Cappello, but she had recently told Matt she would not run again. She was going back to her job at the university, something to do with maps. The geography department, he supposed. What went on there? What could be the contemporary study of geography? Surely everything to be known already was? Matt often found people as smart as Alessandra — intellectual types — tiresome, but she was charming. She never seemed to lose her patience and never condescended to her fellow councillors even when she set them straight. She was a small woman. Her hair was as black as any he'd seen, shot through with grey. She didn't bother dying it. She kept it short. There was faint chevron bridging her eyebrows and a feathery line like shade on her jaw that women usually removed. Matt guessed that most women of Italian descent had her large smoky eyes. He would miss her during the next term. He was going to run again, likely unopposed by a serious contender, if only because he couldn't think what else he might do.

The dress Alessandra had worn to the last council meeting looked very smart, Matt thought, with big, floppy, cloth buttons down the front, like blossoms, like the sort of wild roses you saw along the roadside, and a wide belt. The fabric was tweedy — he didn't know what you called it — and in a cheerful lemon colour. There was often a sense of fun about how she dressed. From his chair in the council chamber he could watch her without being seen to do so. She constantly fought a desire to fidget but couldn't keep her feet in her shoes, always unconsciously letting them slip off before pushing her toes back into them again. Where did she say it was in Italy that she was from? He'd like to go to Italy. Her ankles. Supposing, if she was lying on a bed, on her back on a bed, and he took one of Alessandra's ankles so lightly in his hand. He would lift it and gently push it back. She would open up.

Patty placed her hand on his chest above his heart and pressed down. She moved on to him and put her leg over his.

They didn't make love as much as they used to. Matt couldn't recall the last time she'd initiated it.

She slid her hand down over his belly and found his cock. Matt was only then aware of how hard he was. Patty gave him an especially violent squeeze and then cradled it as if to judge its weight.

"There," she whispered.

She kissed him now, pecking and grazing his lips with her teeth. Then her tongue was against his. She climbed on him, saddling his big thighs and grinding in, reliable and familiar.

He put his hands on her waist and lifted her, still as slight as she was in high school, so that she moved effortlessly over him, almost floating there, gliding in the air above. It was a thing they'd learned to do together.

But now Patty was pushing herself off and sitting up in the bed.

"What is it?" asked Matt.

"I want to pray."

"Sorry . . . you want to what?"

"I would like to pray."

"Pray?"

"To give thanks, to ask for blessing. It's beautiful, sex. It's a sacrament."

"Okay."

"I think it is. I think I love sex."

"I'm glad."

"No, I mean, I like it more this way."

In the dark Matt could see she'd clasped her hands. He supposed her lips were moving, saying a grace of sorts.

NINE

BIRCHES WERE ENCROACHING on and compromising the one-time railway bed. Creases in their papery bark looked to have been drawn in charcoal crayon, the branches and their coin-sized leaves raised a jade scrim.

The tree-lined route followed the river closely enough that the water was always within sight and earshot.

One of the men observed that it was how he imagined Russia—birchy and burbling. The other man offered that he had once been, but was obliged to remain within the city limits of what was then called Leningrad and had not seen the countryside. They were walking against the river's flow, up from the harbour toward Bowring Park.

Their dogs turned on the sound in the same instant. The men heard nothing but knew to trust the animals and looked down the line the two crackies pointed into the brush.

You would expect a man to crash and thrash through growth of such density, but this fellow's passage was swift and easy. Clothes in tatters, he'd bound across the path before it occurred to the dogs to set upon him. He was over the stream as lightly as a skipping stone and with a pace that put the soft townie hounds off the chase before they'd even reached the watercourse.

TEN

IT WAS UNLIKE Mayor Olford to be late, so Alessandra assumed he had other business and couldn't make the Parks and Public Spaces Committee meeting. The free chair at the conference table was next to hers. Terry Durnford, director of planning, was in Matt's usual seat. Durnford went to get up when Matt entered but Matt gestured that Durnford should stay put.

"We started," said Alessandra.

"Of course, my mistake, lost track of time. Continue."

"The matter of the new park off Kavanagh Court," Alessandra told him.

While taking the seat on her left Matt heavily shouldered Alessandra. "Excuse me," he said.

His humility hid considerable physical presence, she thought. This man was once a professional athlete. It was the first thing people in the city knew about him. Alessandra arrived in Canada after his career had ended. Even if she bothered to watch sports she would never have seen him playing his game. Why hadn't she moved her chair to make space for him? How could she not have taken better measure of Matt? Today, he seemed a mountain.

"Yes. Kavanagh Court. Where are we?" he asked.

"My view is that it's better to first establish the" — Alessandra searched for the word — "footprint of what we are going to identify as a 'park' and let it be used, see how people use it, before we 'make' it."

With heavy exhalation of breath, Planning Durnford let everyone know he was unimpressed. Durnford was one of those senior civil servants for whom the trappings of democracy were a nuisance, a needless accounting to the rabble. He was a prickly princess who, when questioned, was given to bureaucratic tantrums. His passive aggression was manifested in incessant, by-the-book consultation with his masters. If you troubled Planning Durnford, he would never stop sending you reports for approval. Durnford owned a shrug of exasperation, a lifting and pinching of the shoulders that said, "I am constrained by idiots." Once cultivated, the gesture became a tic permanently recorded in the fabric of the shoulders of his jackets, crenulated folds now always framed his head. Alessandra would be happy to let Matt deal with him.

"I'm not sure . . . my fault, I came late," said Matt.

"You are always making the point, Councillor Cappello," Durnford spoke, "that we have to be mindful that Bowring Park was designed by Frederick Todd, to respect his work, and here you are now saying that in the case of Kavanagh Court you are against . . . what? Mapping out some paths?"

"But this isn't a proposal for a park designed by a landscape architect, is it? It's an arbitrary pattern of trails, a generic play-ground, a few benches."

"It's Kavanagh Court, Councillor Cappello, and the green space is an afterthought."

"The park was not part of the original development?" asked Matt.

"No, and there's no budget allocation. But there has been a lot of youth crime so..." Alessandra did not finish.

"And this will help?" asked Matt

Nobody seemed to know the answer. Alessandra sensed that it would. Had she read it somewhere? She felt foolish not having something to cite, specific evidence to back up the proposition. Perhaps a park would only give the trouble-makers shelter, make the situation in the grim development worse? Perhaps the problem was the socio-economics of this new trouble spot, the impoverished suburb. Maybe, once the poorly built houses, each indistinguishable from the next, were so carelessly thrown up, Kavanagh Court's fate was sealed.

"Let me get some literature" — Alessandra saw Durnford roll his eyes for the back rows as she said this — "about this, about public spaces finding their own design, and I'll bring some case studies to the next meeting."

"Case studies?" said Durnford.

"That's a good idea," said Matt. "Moving on."

"Nasal are wondering if there might be sections of the city's public spaces set aside for the pollen sensitive community..."

"Nasal?" Matt didn't seem to know what Durnford was talking about.

"The Newfoundland and Labrador Sinus Alliance. NALSL.

They were wondering if there could be parts of the city's parks and other public spaces set aside that were not planted with flowers or trees whose pollen is particularly bothersome."

"Bothersome?" Matt still seemed confused.

"As bothersome as other plants." Durnford looked at a sheet of paper. "They don't like alders or ash trees. Don't like daisies or sunflowers. In terms of grasses... fescue is bad. Their members are allergic..."

"Hay fever... bad hay fever, serious symptoms." This was said by a staffer, Julia Fahey. Alessandra could not remember her title. She looked and sounded like a girl not a woman, dressed to accentuate it. Alessandra wished she would do otherwise.

"They argue that since we provide scent-free change rooms at municipal recreation facilities we should accommodate people who are sensitive to pollen in our public spaces," said Durnford.

Alessandra watched Matt turn his head toward the window. He was either considering the issue or whether he could speak his mind.

"Cannot argue that point, I suppose," he said. "Is this viable?"

Julia had an answer ready. "Crocuses, daffs, periwinkle are better. Grasses, we are still looking into."

"Very well," said Matt. "Next?"

"The man living in Bowring Park," said Durnford.

"So, it's not a band of gypsies?" said Matt.

"No," said Julia, "it is a single male individual. I don't think you can call people gypsies anymore, Your Worship."

"He is like . . . a homeless person?" asked Matt.

"Obviously, sort of, but he's not homeless. We know his name." Julia read from a document. "Harry Davenant, fifty-seven years old. He maintains a residence on Cochrane Street. Rental. Landlord has postdated cheques to next April."

"I know that name," said Alessandra. "He was the artistic director of the LSPU Hall Theatre. He's living in Bowring Park?"

"That is the case," said Durnford.

"I'm missing something," Matt said.

"We don't know why he's living in the park," said Julia. "He's not communicative."

"This is a mental health issue?" Alessandra asked.

"He was working for Sentry Security," said Durnford. "He was making his rounds one night and decided to stay. Sentry has fired him, so now, any time after the park closes at 10 p.m., he's trespassing."

"Call the police," said Matt.

"It's a mental health issue," said Alessandra.

"They'll take care of that," Matt said. "I'm sure more than half of the calls the police take turn out to be mental health issues. If this man is unwell they will get him help."

"That is the plan," said Durnford.

"There are two people who know Mr. Davenant who wanted to meet with you concerning his situation," said Julia.

"Meet?" said Matt.

"Meet councillors on the committee. So you and Councillor Cappello, I guess. Councillor Neary if he'd attended but . . ."

Matt looked at Alessandra again.

"Sure," Alessandra said. "When?"

"They're here. They're in the building. They wanted to see you right after the committee meeting," said Julia.

"Could they not have made an appointment?" Matt asked.

"They could, I suppose," said Julia. "They're here now."

"Okay, have them meet us in my office when we are done," said Matt. "I didn't see the agenda. What else do we have?"

MATT BID THE three go ahead of him. The mayor's office was furnished with a small couch and two chairs, fitted into a corner, for such meetings. The woman introduced herself as Natalie Sommerville. She was a towering figure, with several inches on the bald man, Lloyd Purcell, with whom she'd come, and Purcell was probably six feet tall. Alessandra took Ms. Sommerville to be in her thirties, Purcell closing on fifty.

Sommerville took one chair and Purcell the other, so that Matt was again sitting next to Alessandra on the couch. Alessandra thought they must look like a couple at home hosting visitors.

"We are two of Mr. Davenant's many, many friends. Dear friends," said Natalie Sommerville. Alessandra thought Sommerville strangely attired. She had on high-top sneakers with a long ladder of laces, such as a boxer might wear, and her khaki skirt had odd Velcro-hatched pockets. Her tight, fitted coat was of a shiny, even shimmering, ruby-hued synthetic. Her long brown hair needed brushing. "We presume to represent his interests where he has decided to no longer speak for himself."

"You 'presume'?" Alessandra asked.

"We heard," Matt said, "that he was uncommunicative."

"We believe that silence is his choice and his right," Sommerville said.

"What's wrong with him? Do they know?" Matt asked.

"'Wrong' with him?" Sommerville said.

"He's not ill?" asked Alessandra.

"And who is 'they'?" Sommerville said.

"Can we please start again," Matt said. Alessandra thought, yes, that's the thing to do, start again. "Mr. Davenant is in the middle of some sort of episode and . . ."

"No," said Sommerville, "he is transitioning."

"I don't know the . . . the psychiatric terminology," Matt said.

"You see, even saying 'psychiatric,' that's pathologizing him." It was the first thing Purcell had said. "That's like saying he's species dysphoric. That's not what's going on here."

Alessandra wasn't quick to read people, but something about Matt's expression, almost squinting as if he was trying to focus, told her he didn't trust this Lloyd Purcell character. Purcell kept looking about the office, either to avoid Matt's eye or to take some kind of inventory. Now the woman was saying something. Alessandra wasn't following.

"Transitioning to . . . ?" she asked.

"To a deer," Sommerville said.

Alessandra saw that Natalie Sommerville and Lloyd Purcell expected, even relished, the silence that greeted this proposition.

Purcell's jacket was tailored, a broad check of powdery blue ghosting the navy wool. Good wool too, she saw. And his shirt was colourfully and asymmetrically striped. Façonnable, Alessandra guessed, if not something made. Yes, it was a custom-made shirt. Yet his clothes were a full size too large for him. He was bulky, but not so long ago he'd been even bigger. He was affecting gravity, but Matt did not look convinced. Purcell was a bad actor.

"A deer, like the animal, a deer?" Matt asked.

"Yes," said Purcell. "Deer, like the ruminant mammal."

"*Cervo*," Alessandra said to herself.

"We don't have deer in Newfoundland," said Matt.

"Caribou are of the deer family," Purcell said.

"And moose are the largest member of the deer family," Sommerville said. "And they are plentiful."

"Moose aren't native," Matt said.

"Ms. Sommerville isn't either. She's from Ontario," Purcell said.

"What's that got to do with it?" Matt asked.

"She wouldn't have known," said Purcell, "that moose were introduced to the island."

"I confess I did not know that," said Sommerville.

"*Momento*," said Alessandra. "Sorry, I'm confused. He, Mr. Davenant, thinks he's a deer?"

"He is becoming," said Sommerville, "the deer that was always in him. It's impossible to say if he's a red-tailed or a caribou, and those labels have no meaning. He is foraging. If you saw his locomotion, you'd see."

"To be honest," said Purcell, "I was skeptical until I saw him on the move."

"Is he...like...on all fours?" Matt asked.

"No," said Sommerville, "he's bipedal. But locomotion is only one aspect of who or what one is."

"Like DNA," said Alessandra.

"Is DNA destiny, a dictate?" Purcell seemed to ask himself, as though he was taking note of something he would later research.

"Has a doctor looked at him?" Matt asked.

"This is what we need to talk about," said Sommerville. "Why does a doctor have to come into this?"

"Excuse me, but," Matt said, "if he thinks he is a deer, then he's crazy."

"Why?" asked Sommerville.

"Because he isn't a deer."

"So, if you judge he's 'crazy,' your word. . ." said Purcell. Alessandra saw Matt wince; he knew you couldn't say 'crazy' anymore. "So what?"

"He needs help of some sort, surely." Alessandra felt she should come to Matt's aid.

"He needs help to be who he wants to be. Who he always was," said Sommerville.

"Or might have been," said Purcell, "if allowed. He has sovereignty over his body. "

Alessandra wanted to laugh and bit down against the urge. She must watch herself. The Sommerville woman seemed genuinely concerned about her friend.

"Of course," Alessandra said, "that's his right, I suppose. But whatever is going on, it is going on in a public space. I don't think anyone would quarrel with his choices to do whatever he likes in private, to be a deer in his own home . . . or in his own backyard, I guess. The issue for the city is the park, not Mr. Davenant."

"That's where it gets sticky," Purcell said. "His choice is to range. That's critical to the life he is now living."

"Free range," Sommerville said.

Alessandra now sensed this wasn't going to be a small problem.

"Let's make an important distinction," Purcell continued, "between 'living as' and 'lifestyle.'"

Matt put his two hands in front of him, palms out as if he were pushing something away. Not for the first time Alessandra noticed how wrecked they were. The fingers did not run straight and the knuckle of the index finger of his right hand seemed displaced.

"Okay, stop this now," he said. "I'm not going to argue about the nature of Mr. Davenant's problem or —"

Sommerville tried to interject but Matt anticipated her and kept going.

"— or whether you even consider that he has 'a problem.' Seems semantics to me. Whatever the case, he is remaining in the park after it is closed to the public and that's trespassing, even if he thinks he's a deer. The normal course of action would be to call the police. Would you rather we called a doctor?"

"I guess that's for you to decide," Sommerville said. "We've brought the situation, as we understand it, to your attention. We would like him to be left alone."

"Does this have anything to do with the closure of the LSPU Hall Theatre?" asked Alessandra.

Sommerville looked to Purcell, who shook his head. "Unrelated," Purcell said.

Sommerville rose, followed by Purcell.

"We are trying to do what's best for everyone," Sommerville said.

"He's harming no one out there. He spooks easily, so scarcely anyone has even noticed him. He's disappeared in the trees before they can get a good look at him," Purcell said.

"So he's shy," said Matt.

"Skittish," Purcell replied.

"People want a selfie with him," said Sommerville. "Well meaning, I know, but inappropriate."

They all shook hands and Sommerville and Purcell left.

Matt stood and crossed the office to his desk, pacing a circle in front of it.

"'Did you hear that? 'Trying to *do* what's best.' Heed that, it's a warning sign, Councillor."

"A warning of what?"

"A warning that busybodies are on the loose. A deer! Jaysus."

"It is, on the face of it, it is silly but..."

"Don't worry, Councillor Cappello, I've learned to be careful. Jumped through hoops for that transgendered dispatcher up at the city depot."

"I don't know about her."

"No, him. Was her, now him. Bryce. Why anyone would go with 'Bryce' is a job to say."

"Wasn't there a transgendered constabulary officer?"

"That was a her — Trevor to Trudy," said Matt. "Victim of her own success; nobody made a fuss until she started getting promoted. Former male colleagues resented that she was benefiting from affirmative action..."

"As would women on the force."

"More so, they were livid. Kept catcalling her, pointing downstairs. What was it they said? ... 'Uter*us*.' It got so uncomfortable for her at the cop shop that she quit. Works for some corporate security outfit down in the States. Arizona, I think. Wasn't hard to look at."

"Matt!"

"And in the uniform, hot as balls..."

"Stop!" Alessandra said. Matt made her laugh.

"What are you going to do?" she asked.

"Nothing. I will let the security people call the police. A doctor will look at him and put him in the hospital; it's right across the street from the park."

"It's so primitive, isn't it? Health care for mental illness? They don't even know what the mind is, let alone how to treat it. What will they do for this man, really?"

"They'll try to help him. They do their best. I like to think they do." Matt sat on the front edge of his desk. The problem seemed to have tired him out of all proportion. His ruined paws were gripping the desk with unwarranted vigour. Alessandra saw Matt trace her gaze back to his hands.

"Hockey."

"I'm sorry...I've always worried you were in an accident. Was I staring?"

"Yes, you were staring. I'm used to it." Matt smiled to tell Alessandra that he didn't care if she looked. "Sticks and pucks had a way of finding this hand." Matt let loose his left hand's hold on the desk. "I was sort of a faceoff specialist so.... You know what a faceoff is?"

"No, I don't," said Alessandra.

Matt laughed and lit up, as if Alessandra's ignorance of hockey was the best news he'd heard all day.

"It's when they drop the puck, to start play?"

Alessandra nodded. This she knew.

"So I was always putting my hand in harm's way," said Matt, "sticking it into a thresher. Everybody has a target painted on them somewhere, right?"

Alessandra thought about this assertion. It wasn't true. Was it? And if so, where was hers?

"And I permanently fucked — sorry, *injured* — the knuckle in a fight."

"Right. There's a lot of fighting in hockey."

"It wasn't my thing. Single racket my entire NHL career."

"That's where you broke your knuckle?" Alessandra winced to think of it.

"No. That was in Quebec Major Junior. It's like a minor league that feeds into The Bigs. I fought there. Had to. It was part of the test."

"So you didn't enjoy it, fighting?"

"Not at all. Despite the game's reputation, there aren't many players who enjoy it. It's a job for some, a chore. It's part of the show. It's foolish to even call it fighting, it's mostly flailing."

"Show?"

"Yeah, it's entertainment, popular entertainment. At the professional level it's about the commercials, about the beer and the pickup trucks. It's a show."

Alessandra watched Matt examine the old wound, recalling, she saw, the conflict, where and when and how it occurred.

"Yep, this joint gave way fracturing the 'zygomatic process' of a guy from Finland, a decent prospect named Rejo Avenen." Making a loose fist, Matt put the knuckle against his own cheekbone to illustrate the blow to the Finn's face. "He lost sight in the eye."

"Oh my. For how long?"

"Forever. That was his last hockey game. With that eye gone he had no depth perception. And I lost the fight. Badly. Got shit-knocked. You don't see the Finns fight a lot, but this Avenen was a savage. He was one of those few players who relished a racket and then, in the end..."

"Fighting is..." Alessandra couldn't think what fighting *was*.

"That guy," Matt looked toward the door. He was done talking about his past.

"Lloyd Purcell. What did you make of him?"

"Seemed...normal to me, certainly not hysterical. Seemed reasonable. Do you know his story?"

"Name is vaguely familiar. I'll google it."

"Did you notice his clothes?" asked Alessandra.

"You know, I did! And I usually don't."

"The jacket was definitely made...you know, by a tailor. And the shirt too; it had French seams."

"That means nothing to me."

"Stitching; it's boring. Something that someone who knows clothes would ask for. We Italians...it matters to us more than it should."

"He didn't seem like someone who 'knew clothes.' He looked rocky to me."

"Maybe a borrowed jacket?"

Matt shrugged. "I shop at Moores."

"And you always look "—Alessandra knew the word she was looking for—"sharp."

"Thank you."

"I should be going. My husband, Jules, he's not well and it's not safe to leave him alone too long."

"Audrey told me he was ill, had to leave work. He's a professor at the university, isn't he? The big John Cabot expert?"

"That is he."

"So, taking early retirement?"

"No. No, it's not early."

ELEVEN

NATALIE SOMMERVILLE AND Lloyd Purcell stepped from City Hall into a cloudless day.

"They are clearly hostile to the proposition," Purcell said.

"They were not open to it, but they were not entirely closed. The mayor seemed interested," said Natalie. "I'm hopeful."

"I've been to a lot of pitches, Natalie, and you get a sense when people are not liking what they are hearing. The mayor, Olford, is a very backward guy"—Lloyd Purcell fished his pockets for something—"really conservative you know. Was a hockey player."

"I didn't know that."

"Oh yeah, that's how he got elected." Purcell donned the sunglasses he'd found, an act that calmed him. "Was on some big NHL team, out in Alberta, I think...and not an important player, but a Newfoundlander making good on the mainland, a local boy. Those are his only qualifications."

"It's her that worries me," said Natalie.

"Cappello?"

"That's her name, Cappello? Makes sense; they're swarthy aren't they, Italians."

"I don't follow."

"She would do well to see an aesthetician."

"I didn't notice," said Lloyd.

"You said that Harry's transitioning was unrelated to him losing his job at the theatre?"

"Is there a connection?"

"I don't know," said Natalie.

"Okay, I should have said, 'We don't know.'"

"I'm going to the park to try and see him tomorrow," she said. "Do you want to come along?"

"I would, but tomorrow I can't. I have something to do for my brother in the morning and then a call to Los Angeles in the afternoon, business... it's their morning."

"Of course. I guess you couldn't be farther away from Los Angeles, could you?"

"No, I couldn't. You're right about that. Are you going...?" Lloyd Purcell gestured eastward, down Duckworth Street.

"Yes."

"Then I shall leave you here. Post office," he said. "Call me and tell me how it goes in the park."

"I will."

Natalie watched Lloyd cross the road, dodging traffic, and head south toward Water Street. They'd met at a bar downtown where she had gone to see a band she mistakenly assumed played Celtic music. It was, instead, a sort of jazz that flirted with howling lunacy. But the music clearly moved Lloyd and that openness to passion made him attractive to her. Most of the men with whom she'd been seemed to lose interest in life. She needed enthusiasm. And Lloyd was an interesting man. He was in the movie business for years, on a first-name basis with stars, and gave it all up to come home to Newfoundland.

Though from Toronto, Natalie thought she probably knew better than Lloyd himself what drew people back to this island. The place was enchanted. Locals, even those as sensitive as Lloyd, were inured to it, so long were they inside the mystery they could not see how it acted upon them.

Natalie came to St. John's to organize local protests against the seal hunt, only to discover that the taking of the baby white coats had ceased many years earlier and that the remaining hunt, for older animals, was negligible. While visiting the university's marine biology research station a few kilometres outside the town, Natalie had since seen, up close, adult harp and hood seals and found them repulsive. They were so much larger than she expected, monstrous almost, and given to surly, fishy flatulence. The seal's was the reverse of man's condition, of being so hideous in infancy and growing into beauty. Natalie thought human babies unspeakably ugly, no better than swollen, squirming spermatozoa with the unfortunate habit of suckling.

Natalie never used the return portion of her airline ticket. Since her decision to stay in Newfoundland, she had met some of the few natives who did perceive the magic of their land, who were *open*, who told her tales of those from "the shore" who'd been fairy-led, of children born with canine teeth and emerging from the womb singing in an unknown tongue. Fergus, whom she'd met at O'Leary's on open-mic night, told the most amazing tales of banshees and boodarbies that lived "up the Horsechops," of people hexed. Fergus was only last month arrested on trumped-up pederasty charges that his friends at the pub said were payback for his having figured out a way to game the Employment Insurance program. Under his system, Fergus merely got himself fired upon reporting for work on a shrimper to Greenland drunk and then collecting benefits for many months.

Natalie thought she herself might be picking up a hint of the local brogue.

Lloyd was wrong about the mayor having been elected because of his athletic fame. Natalie saw it was because he was gorgeous; the full, ungovernable chestnut hair, the wide mouth and sturdy jaw. His eyes were too dark to be called brown; they were black coffee. There was only a tiny scar to mar that face, a jag on his left cheek. His hands were not attractive; she'd almost call one of them, she couldn't recall if it was his right or left, mangled. It looked like it belonged to an aged labourer with an injury that had not properly healed or set. Still, he was strikingly handsome and with the added charm of his not really caring that he was. The mayor's good looks made Natalie warm to him. There was nothing for it; Natalie was a tall girl and liked a big man such as the mayor.

Through the space between two buildings piled into the hill she could see the harbour below, an unstained supply vessel from the offshore oil play seemingly drifting, sliding through the placid water with the grace of a whale, awaiting a berth perhaps, and then beyond it the South Side hills, steeper than the shore she was on and verdant, like a ruin wall claimed by climbing vines and moss. She was right, she was; they couldn't see it, the locals, in the same way they failed to notice the mood-altering fog and ceaseless wind.

She stopped for an early lunch at The Sprout, a vegetarian restaurant. Staff waved to her as she took her regular seat. It was true what they said about Newfoundlanders being friendly. Their hearts were large. They were, even if they didn't know it, liberal. Lloyd was wrong about Mayor Olford; the citizenry wouldn't go in for someone who was "backward." These Newfoundland people would be sympathetic to what Harry Davenant was going through, even if they didn't understand it.

Natalie was going to be careful; she knew if she moved too quickly the idea would seem strange. Surely anyone who had a pet knew that other species were not unknowable solitudes. Natalie watched documentaries where animals of different species, raised together, cared for each other. Tigers and bears and lions could be siblings, lovingly grooming one another, frolicking together even. Natalie once heard an owl in Algonquin Park and picked her way through the forest to find it in a raggedy pine and when it looked down at her there was a mutual acknowledgement. There was. She'd told her sister, Martha, the story and was mocked for it.

She knew crows mourned their dead, crowded the perches above their fallen, their knowing and feeling souls setting them to nodding and a joining in a cacophony of keening. This was fact!

She envied Harry's courage. She had never felt any deer-like stirrings, but maybe something canine. She'd looked a fox in the eye out at Cape Spear while feeding it (despite posted signs prohibiting her from doing so) and felt a connection as strong as she had to any person. Perhaps it was her native heritage. She'd recently discovered that her maternal great-grandmother might have been one part half-blood Tuskaweegee, a fact Natalie honoured with a tattoo on her lower back.

Lloyd said there was nothing remotely cervine (Lloyd knew that word; he was that sort of man) about Harry before he began his change. Lloyd said Harry was actually lead-footed and graceless for an actor and that's why he'd ended up in the administration end of theatre. But Harry was deer-like now; there was no mistaking it when you saw him. She thought that Lloyd noticed Harry's deer nature first, but Lloyd assured her it was she, and now, thinking back, she saw Lloyd was right.

Natalie looked at the menu. She wanted a Black-Bean Burrito but the last one she ate made her gassy. She decided instead on the Tempeh Tantrum, which was also delicious.

TWELVE

FIDDLER'S WAS A real bar, blessedly a mere thirty thirsty paces from the front doors of City Hall, yet far enough that Natalie was safely out of sight when Lloyd entered. A cold beer in the middle of the day in a proper drinking establishment — there was nothing like it. That one could no longer enjoy a cigarette at the same time would spoil the experience in a lesser place. Only a stone's throw away was the block of yeast known as George Street; joints from the same faux-Celtic pub kit, "Mussels in the Corner" on an endless loop, cod-kissing rubes from the mainland and soused locals looking to fuck or fight. Further east along Duckworth and Water Streets, noxious winey places were popping up like mushrooms to accommodate the young and dissipated of the oil boom. How could anyone aspire to be a yuppie after they'd seen that shit show in the '80s? Thanks be to Jesus for Fiddler's and the Sports Club up on Boncloddy Street.

Lloyd had told Natalie that he was going to the post office

and here, next to him, belly to the bar, was an actual postman, in uniform, having a rum and Coke. That alone made it right. The proprietor fancied the place a sort of museum and filled it with Newfoundland bric-a-brac on that theme alone, without another governing principle — here a rusting two-handed crosscutter from the lumberwoods, there a harpoon, here a gaff for busting open the skulls of seals. It was beautiful.

THIRTEEN

"...I'M HOLDING FOR Staff Inspector Leigh. It's Inspector Gary Mackenzie of the Royal Newfoundland Constabulary. Yes... I was just... Royal. Newfoundland. Constabulary. But that's not... hello?   Staff Inspector Leigh? Yeah, sure, 'Peter,' gotcha. Hello, thanks for taking... Yeah. No, no not St. John, New Brunswick. St. John's, Newfoundland. John's*sssss*. Pardon me? Yeah, I was with Toronto Police. For years. Long story. Riiiight.   No, I did not know what I was thinking. So did you...? Okay, thanks.   They were protesting stray cats and dogs being euthanized at the city's shelter here, no, no not a big deal and nobody made trouble but I saw the name Natalie Sommerville on the list and it... it was familiar, yeah, rung a bell. So, yeah, my concern was animal rights, extreme you know, so ALF or ARM, but there's nothing on any national database.   No. Something twigged. Okay. Okay. *Sommerville*, two Ms, two Ls. Natalie Sommerville. I can call back. Okay, that's great.   Thanks. No... go ahead.

G20? Right. No. Makes sense. Yeah. No, that's good, we're all good. Thanks, Peter."

Gary Mackenzie hung up, recalling and worrying now — from the knowing look the Sommerville woman had given him, the way their eyes met, however briefly, across the small parking lot in front of the city pound — that she'd recognized him from his undercover work during the G20 protests back in 2010.

FOURTEEN

WALLY'S QUAD: an RZR 900 Polaris Pursuit. In Camo. Loves it.
Shag the tree-huggers of downtown St. John's, that crowd
of comefromaways in designer rubber boots. What did Cy
Jardine call them? "The bellyaching Veggie Burghers of the
East End." They complained that the machines destroyed the
country! But it wasn't their country. It was Wally's. Wally's
dad's. A giant, his dad, Brendan. Respected. Feared. Up the
whole Southern Shore. And this was their land, regardless of
what the Crown said. If they wanted to drive a quad up here or
over the Perroquet Downs or through the Avalon *Wilderness*
Area that was their business. Masterless. They'd thrown off
the Englishman's shackles and made their own way on these
bogs, in these woods. Jesus, one day the O'Neills are resettled
out of Dunchy Head and the next persecuted for keeping a spot
up in the country to snare a few rabbits.

Not long after WestJet established a service between St.
John's and Dublin, Wally took a pilgrimage to the ancestral

home. But he found Dublin grubby and sour, a pricey international anywhere. His Irish brethren were completely uninterested when he mentioned Newfoundland's connection. The pubs looked exactly like their knock-offs back in St. John's and the Guinness didn't taste any better. It tasted the same. Wally was happy to come home out of it. He was a true Newfoundlander.

On his favourite route for the quad there was a minty tunnel made by low-hanging larch branches that Wally loved shooting through. Rocketing out the end of it the four-wheeler came right off the ground and didn't she bounce like a rubber ball when she came down again. Almost lost control of the machine every time, Wally did.

Clearing the stand of trees he tore across a pelt of barrens, the pond they called Skin Tilt in his sights.

His father, Big Brendan, had expected more of Wally, Wally knew. He could be mayor of St. John's but for Matt Olford. Hey, the guy won a Stanley Cup with the Oilers, wore the ring. Not that Olford did much with that team; he was, like, third or fourth line. But Olford had played enough hockey to get elected.

Olford had figured out the municipal politics game too, how to remain in office as long as he wanted: do nudding, do dick-all and take no stand. Previous mayors worked themselves into a lather dealing with the mini-mayors of the outlying communities, the tax-avoiding brown-baggers, trying to get them to grow up on issues of infrastructure and sharing the burden. When they told Olford they wouldn't pay he shrugged and said he understood their position. Six months later they were asking him how to spend the money they'd begged from the province or the feds. Olford let them come to him with solutions it should have been his business to imagine. Wally couldn't operate like that; he couldn't sit still. He was a doer.

By now Wally should have gotten the call from Whassiname McAvoy, should have been courted to stand for Parliament as the Member for St. John's South and, by default, being the only federal Conservative from Newfoundland, be destined for the Cabinet of the Government of Canada. Privy Councillor. That's how Brendan laid it out for him. But Wally got tangled up in that moose thing, shot a cow with a "bull only" licence and got nailed by Wildlife on the road out. He knew Bill Murphy kept a moose cock in his freezer for such a possibility but that day, that one day, Wally neglected to take the dong along.

The Liberal Party had recently sent a messenger to indicate they could forgive and forget but they weren't going anywhere. Wally wasn't going to be a sacrificial lamb.

So now Wally "Bull Only" O'Neill was a city councillor and his brother, Des, ran the Blackmarsh Inn. They were small-time. And with all this prosperity, all the new money—it was galling. This was their time to be in on the action and they were outside the tent. They were outside the gravel pit camp! They were with the bears up to the fucking dump!

Everybody else was getting rich from the oil play. Everybody else was getting a piece. You needed money to make money. He and Des had an idea, a solid idea for a new evacuation system for the offshore rigs. Wally was going to take it to Gerald Hayden, was waiting on a meeting. He was going to get the O'Neills back in the game.

He stopped the quad next to the water and turned her off. It was quiet but for the whinging of a faraway chainsaw. When his father brought Des and he here as boys it took a few hours to walk in. The pond was blocked with fair-sized mud trout then. It was fished out now.

Wally lit a Player's Light. That was his reward, a smoke. These days a man had to skulk off to the woods to enjoy a dart without being harassed.

The fisheries had come and gone and fortunes were made. Wally's people were the ones in the longliners and the trawlers, the ones swept overboard, lost at sea, the ones bent and broken by toil, and when it was said and done and the cod were gone the O'Neills were back where they started. Wally wasn't going to let it happen again.

He flicked the butt into the pond and started up the machine. Its guts and his were one.

The existing ATV tracks leading up from the beach were so deeply cut into the peat that tea-coloured water was pooling in them. They were too greasy for purchase so he broke new trail. The machine's front wheels clawed up over the bank with a roar that raised a fox hiding in the tuckamore. The animal was sooty and silver, with what looked to be black leggings like a baseball player might wear. The fleet creature made for the trees. Wally went for it with the quad, gunning the engine.

FIFTEEN

PATTY DIDN'T PROSELYTIZE and never once asked Matt to accompany her to a service. She'd joined the church of her own accord; she was never recruited. She reported to Matt that she accepted an invitation to attend a service as a courtesy and had a much more pleasant experience than she expected. The things she heard there made sense, she said. She went back again unbidden. She was insistent that no one tried to "convert" her. She sent their children religious material, but never showed any of it to Matt.

Patty did send Matt annoying motivational e-cards: a picture of a mountaineer on a summit with the word "AMBITION" and some drippy message imploring the reader to get on with it. Today she had posted, on her Facebook page, one of those takes on the "Keep Calm and Carry On" posters from the Blitz; the crown at the top of the card was replaced with a crucifix and the message below said "Keep Calm and Rely Upon."

How was Matt supposed to respond?

Stranger than these new messages was that Patty used to, not so long ago, post the mock versions. An image of hands stacked at the centre of a huddle with the caption "Meetings: Because none of us is as dumb as all of us." An image of charging bulls closing on a Pamplona runner with the caption "Tradition: Doesn't mean it's not stupid."

Could someone block irony, make themselves deaf to something they'd always heard? Maybe the sense could be lost through exposure to excessive sarcasm or in a single blast of ridicule too cruel.

Patty was the office manager at Atlantech Petroleum Services. She worked alongside engineers, perhaps not scientists, but empiricists, men and women of fact, of measure, more than of faith. What exactly had his wife—whom he loved, who was always so much more intelligent and skeptical than he—chosen?

He'd opened his laptop to google "Lloyd Purcell" and had seen the "Keep Calm and Rely Upon" Facebook posting, as had, he realized, his neck reddening, many, many others. What were her colleagues at work saying? Their friends? What were their friends saying about Pats and Matt? *"She left him for Jesus!"* *"Hush, Alan, that's a terrible thing to say."*

He typed "Lloyd Purcell" into the search box. There was a Wikipedia page and an IMDB page, which Matt saw was something to do with the film and television business. He remembered hearing about the guy now. He was a writer in Hollywood and got into trouble down there, something sordid to with drugs or boys or girls. Yes, Lloyd Purcell's brother— Matt could not remember his name—ran a restaurant on the outskirts of town, in what was now Dewey Mercer's ward, where Matt and Patty and Steve and Belinda once ate a wonderful meal. What was that place called? It was back in the day when going out to eat was about the people with whom you dined, not the chef's IMDB page. Food seemed such a fuss these days, thought Matt.

Matt clicked on the Wikipedia page. It was short and incomplete, as if someone had started it and then abandoned the project. He scrolled down, looking for details about Purcell's run-in with the law in Los Angeles. The guy had worked on a television show, *All Heart*, that Matt had seen, and some movies he thought he might have heard of. Where was Personal Life, he wondered as he scrolled.

Audrey's voice came over the intercom.

"You have a call from the Prime Minister's Office."

Matt depressed the talkback button.

"Who at the Prime Minister's Office?"

"It's a woman, Carole. She's calling for a 'Fred McAvoy.'"

"I think I know that name. Does he have a title?"

"Communications something."

"The Prime Minister's Office?"

"Yes, sir."

"Sure it's not a prank, Audrey?"

"I don't think so."

Matt wondered what it could be, worried he'd forgotten something. He sat on a couple of national bodies to do with municipal governance and they were forever appealing for more federal money.

"Okay, I'll take it."

He picked up the phone handset.

"Hello?"

"Mayor Olford?" It was a woman's voice.

"Yes."

"Please hold for Mr. McAvoy."

Matt supposed he was being asked to join some new committee to do with cities. He wasn't a member of a political party so it wasn't a plum.

"Mayor Olford?"

"Yes."

"Fred McAvoy. I'm with the Prime Minister's Office."

"What can I do for you, Mr. McAvoy?"

"I remember seeing you play with the Oilers."

"Yes?"

"I'm a Leafs fan, even when I lived in Calgary."

"Lotsa Leafs fans out there" — Matt closed his laptop — "despite it all."

"It really must have been something to play for that Oilers squad. The best team ever?"

"The best players on that team were some of the best to ever play the game. But I'm very biased. Case to be made for the 1970 Bruins too, and those Montreal teams a few years later." Matt heard himself talking too much. "The team wasn't better because I was on it, that's for sure."

"Don't be modest. I think you won most of the big faceoffs."

Matt won them all.

"Yes. I'm proud of that." Why was this guy calling? Did Matt remember the name McAvoy from the news?

"Yanic Perreault was a top man on the faceoff, don't you think?"

"Exceptional. If he'd been bigger. In the league, then. He doesn't get the recognition he deserves. Wasn't a terrific skater." Matt thought again he should be listening more closely; there seemed some subtext he was missing. Surely this McAvoy character hadn't called to talk about the finer points of the faceoff. "And Perreault played for some teams... teams in transition."

"'Teams in transition,' yeah. Who was the best—besides yourself, of course—the best on the faceoff?"

"Stan Mikita," answered Matt. Was it a prank? Who was this really?

"Curved blade though. I'd put an asterisk next to everyone on that Chicago team. I never liked them. Bobby Hull—overrated. And a drunk. The prime minister is writing a book about the Leafs. Dave Keon as well, on the faceoff?"

"Yes. But like Mikita, different league than me." Matt disagreed with McAvoy's assessment of a Black Hawks unit he considered one of the greatest.

McAvoy switched to French.

"*Vous avez joué pour une équipe Junior au Québec?*"

"*Oui, à Trois-Rivières, les Draveurs.* Some called them the Dukes."

"*Vous avez... appris le français là-bas?*"

"*C'était ma mineure à l'université, mais oui, le français que j'ai, si c'est bien ça qu'ils parlaient, c'est là que je l'ai appris.*"

"What was your major?" McAvoy returned to English.

"Economics."

Matt thought he heard McAvoy laugh, or make a sound that was meant to be understood as laughter. It was considered and unnatural.

"Now why didn't I know that?" McAvoy said. The comment was directed to someone else too, his mouth was away from the handset. There were others in that room in Ottawa with him. "The prime minister is forever reminding us that he's an economist."

"I'm not an economist. I was an undergraduate. Not really any . . . I don't profess a deep understanding."

"What is it that Keynes said? 'In the end we're all dead.'"

"On his deathbed he said, 'My only regret is that I have not drunk more champagne.'"

"Really?"

"The quote you're thinking of is 'In the long run we are all dead,'" said Matt. "Mostly misunderstood, I think."

"Oh?"

"Yeah. It was to do with economists ignoring the immediate consequences of policy and, you know, thinking about an abstract . . . long term, about the future and not the present. I haven't thought about it in many years."

"Obviously the prime minister's inclinations are to the Freshwater school, common sense really."

"Like I say, I've not put it to much practical use."

"That cannot be true."

"There's scant economic theory running a city — we have few levers to pull. We are at the mercy of larger forces." Matt regretted saying this; it was like he was making excuses.

"You were in business."

"I was in sales. Hayden Heavy Equipment, and truth be told it was the Stanley Cup ring that sold the excavators."

"Gerald Hayden is a significant contributor to the

Conservative Party. He's mentioned you."

"Oh."

"Do you know why I'm calling?"

"No, I do not, Mr. McAvoy."

"Never got wind of any polling?"

"I don't have a big political organization. We're not active between campaigns."

"Our party's research is exceptional. We did some polling in St. John's South."

"Okay?"

"You would win the seat for the Conservative Party."

"I... I'm not... Traditionally in St. John's municipal politics we don't run on a ticket or with a party affiliation, so I..."

"None of the other names even stood a chance. Good names. You're popular. I'm speaking for the prime minister."

"I'm not a member of—"

"Getting a representative in Cabinet from Newfoundland has been a problem for us. It's a priority. Where there is so much growth out there in the resource sector."

"I understand."

"It's not like the price of oil is going anywhere but up."

"No."

"China."

"Yeah, for sure, China."

"Of course, I can't promise..."

"Of course not."

"Our polling indicates you would easily unseat the incumbent and a number of other competitive candidates from the other parties."

"Heartened to know that. I'm not . . . a Conservative."

"You've been a responsible fiscal manager. You are not affiliated with the Liberal Party or the NDP?"

"I am not. Over the years I've been approached by people from all three parties, provincially, hoping I'd run. Gerald Hayden was always trying to sign me up, but I've never seriously considered—"

"It seemed incredible to me."

"What did?"

"That you'd . . . I mean, this far along in a political career and . . . it's so . . . " McAvoy searched for the word. "So *chaste*."

"Politics aren't ideological down here. Its clans and tribes."

"It's the time in the prime minister's mandate to make changes, to bring in new blood. You would be a great addition to our team. I'm speaking for the prime minister."

"I would have thought there'd be someone else already considering a run . . ."

"There is someone—long connections to the Progressive Conservative Party, family connections—but for a number of reasons we can't get into the prime minister doesn't consider him suitable."

". . . I can't give you an answer . . ."

"No, no. I didn't expect one. Think it over."

"I will."

"Not for too long. Please keep our discussion in confidence."

"Absolutely."

"Strict confidence."

"Understood."

"Wayne Gretzky was going to run for us in Toronto but he

would have had to move back to Canada."

"Right."

"Your wife, Patricia, she's a member of the same church as the prime minister — the Christian and Missionary Alliance?"

"Yes, she is. I'm not a member of the church."

"We know."

"And I'm not a member of any church. I'm not...," Matt now said, for the first time in his life, he supposed, "I am not a believer."

A stage laugh. "Perhaps winning St. John's East will make one of you."

"St. John's South."

"Yes. Right you are. More important that you believe in Canada, allegiance to Her Majesty and all that."

"Of course."

"You're not one of those who took down the Canadian flag? No Newfie separatist stuff in the closet?"

"Those people, Mr. McAvoy, they're not serious, they're malcontents."

"If you decide to run there is a background checklist thing. The party uses a company, Dalton Monitor. They'll contact you if they need something clarified."

"I am an open book. Everything you need to know about me is on the back of my hockey card."

McAvoy laughed. It was genuine, spontaneous this time, but it was not pleasing to the ear, ringing where it shouldn't have, as if he were flexing a cramped muscle.

"That's a great line. Great. You're good with the media I bet."

"I haven't been tested."

"You are being modest. Can the prime minister call you some time to talk hockey?"

"If he'd like."

"He would. Think about the offer."

"I will."

"We are going to win the next federal election, Mayor Olford. It's going to be a second strong, stable, majority Conservative government."

Matt was long enough in politics to know this might be true or false, that no one knew.

"Are you . . . I probably shouldn't ask . . ."

"Is the prime minister going to lead the party into the next election?"

"That was my question," said Matt.

"The coming contest will be the most important of our lifetime. The last election was about a return to stability. The ballot question next time out is whether Canada is, as we would argue it always has been, an essentially conservative country, fiscally but more importantly socially. The choices before the voters will be clear. This has been a personal crusade of the prime minister. Once this fundamental question of our true character is resolved, I think only then would the prime minister's greater project be completed to his satisfaction. He's not a coward; he's not going to run from the most important fight in this country's history. "

Matt thought that McAvoy must have said much of this before, so effortlessly did it roll off his tongue.

"Okay."

"Your father was in the RCMP," said McAvoy.

"Yes, he was. Assistant commissioner for B Division. He died in 2007. My mother soon after."

"And she played the piano."

"She did."

"The prime minister likes to play the piano. Talk soon, Matt."

"Goodbye."

Matt put the handset back in its cradle. This was something extraordinary. Wasn't it? The prime minister of Canada was inviting him into government. Matt couldn't be mayor of St. John's forever. That would be sad. Long-term mayoralties always ended in shabby scandal, in pathos. At fifty years, Matt was young enough that a stint in the federal Cabinet would lead to some plum corporate directorships, to making some real money.

What had they said? What had he and McAvoy discussed? Hockey. Faceoffs. Stan Mikita, Yannick Perreault, Dave Keon. They'd polled the riding. Matt's want of belief seemed not to be an issue. Faith in Canada, not Yahweh, was paramount. Naturally. That was easy; Canada was a great place to live, safer and more prosperous than most places. The Queen? "Allegiance to Her Majesty," he'd said. Matt hadn't lied, had he? Yes, he implied fealty to the Crown when he thought it patent nonsense. He thought Elizabeth II possessed no more legitimacy than the Easter Bunny. With whom had he ever shared this thought? Patty. A couple of pals, in passing. It would not haunt him and he never had trouble pretending, swearing oaths in the name of that which he did not believe.

How, Matt wondered, could they even know or care that his mother played the piano? Peculiar.

This was exciting. It was. Economics came up, Freshwater school. Empirical macro, supply-siders, believers in small, non-interventionist government. Matt retained only morsels of knowledge from his half-assed B.A., some obvious truths about supply and demand, but he graduated with the sense that beyond those economics was scarcely more than augury. The prognostications of the foremost experts were wrong more often than right. The financial columns in the business pages of the papers were not so different from those in the sports section, mostly guys talking about anything other than that which actually confronted them and doing so with all the authority of horoscopes and miracle diets. The "economy" was merely a diagnosis of the culture's current state of mind, booming and busting like the cycling between mania and depression, treated as ineffectively by doses of either free or regulated markets. Was it? His economics was as bad as his French. But he wore a Stanley Cup ring.

He pushed the intercom button.

"Mayor Olford?"

"Audrey, could we please not tell anyone about that call."

"Of course not."

"Really, okay?"

"Yes, sir. You've got the private meeting of Council in ten minutes, sir."

"Yes. Thank you," Matt said.

SIXTEEN

"…THEY'D HAVE 'IM now if they'd installed those security cameras." What was Wally O'Neill getting on with? Something to do with the Davenant man in the park? "Motion detectors, right. Can we vote on security cameras again? Fluid situation, right."

"Your heart's in the Highlands, Wally," said Councillor Jardine.

The Conservative Party would raise the money for his campaign, Matt supposed. The call had come from the Prime Minister's Office, after all. They would have a team ready for him. He would require a professionally run organization. That had a cost. The incumbent was not of highest competence but his previous victory was by a fair margin. And while the guy had fumbled a few during his first term in Parliament he had not right out shit the bed. Newfoundlanders were allergic to the governing Conservative Party of Canada. They were, without Matt in the race, unelectable on the island. But the dislike

wasn't substantive. There had been slights and broken prom-
ises, betrayals real but mostly imagined. That was politics. It
was nothing the construction of a new prison in the province
wouldn't solve.

Newfoundlanders could not find a human connection
with the prime minister and so would not trust him. Perhaps
it was merely a cultural difference; the prime minister was
from Ontario via Alberta, so as strange to Newfoundland as
a Dutchman. Polling or no, the campaign would not be, like
his runs at the mayoralty had been, a cakewalk.

Newfoundland had no sway, was a de facto colony of
Canada. They didn't need a seat in Newfoundland. The only
possible concern they could have was the need of someone
in Newfoundland to deliver the message of the multinational
resource companies. They needed an ambassador, a translator.

And Matt wasn't a Conservative. He wasn't anything. He
was suspicious of tribal associations and ideologues; party
politics was a dressing room. But standing for the federal
Conservatives was different than wearing a Tory or Liberal
hat provincially, in Newfoundland. The Conservative Party
of Canada stood for something. Something.

Alessandra looked to be exasperated by whatever it was that
Wally was saying. She was on her feet before Matt acknowledged her.

"Councillor O'Neill, this circumstance changes nothing.
It is the same as it was before. Surveillance cameras invade
everyone's privacy in an effort to catch a small minority com-
mitting some offence, and in this case a man is in the park after
hours. No one has been harmed."

"You know what I don't get? Why would anyone go to a park for privacy? Seems retarded."

"Councillor O'Neill!" Matt said. "You'd wear that word if this was a public meeting."

"Sorry, bad habit. It just come out. I'll stop. If we has security cameras the cops would know where he's to and go get him, obviously they don't have the manpower to be down beating the bushes."

"How is he surviving?" asked Councillor Jardine.

"I suppose he's foraging," said Alessandra. "It's the big thing in gastronomy these days."

"In wha?" said Wally.

"I've heard people are leaving him food," Councillor Dewey Mercer volunteered. "There's a Facebook page. He has a lot of supporters. He thinks he's a deer."

"Who says," asked Councillor Jardine, "that he thinks he's a deer?"

"I heard he's an Englishman," said Wally.

"Assigned 'broke actor' at birth, was he?" said Jardine.

This was a sign, thought Matt. This ridiculous congress, the foolishness now going on in the chamber, was telling him it was time to move on, to take up the prime minister's invitation. These private meetings of city council were ostensibly held to deal with matters that demanded a citizen's confidentiality or a legal shroud but were more often, as was the case now, to spare everyone embarrassment.

Maybe Matt wasn't a Conservative but he was conservative. Sort of. Maybe not. The political parties of the centre and left were confused. Their policies were fuzzy and incoherent.

They had no program. The Liberal Party of Canada was still tainted by scandal and a legacy of cronyism, in such desperate condition they'd resorted to stunt-casting former Prime Minister Pierre Trudeau's son, Justin, as their leader. They were going nowhere for the foreseeable future. The federal New Democratic Party presented itself as progressive to a country that, in its private moments, was not. Ideals were only that: ideals, hopes, and dreams. Matt shared them, wanted the kids with talent to go to music school, wanted another MRI machine for the hospital, wanted public broadcasting, but one had to be practical. Matt was at least a fiscal conservative. Discipline. Balanced books. Economic decisions made in self-interest not only drove the machine, they were almost always more prudent. In that we were pure animals.

If he was going to make a move to federal or provincial politics, now was the time.

"The police have been notified that the gentleman is trespassing," Matt said. "That he thinks he is a deer is, frankly, not the issue."

"He *identifies* as a deer, Your Worship," said Councillor Mercer. "That's what it says on the Facebook page."

"Do you suppose other ruminants think this is cultural... whadda they call it?" Jardine searched for the word. "Appropriation?" No one bothered to hear him.

"We don't have deer in Newfoundland," said Wally.

"I will follow up," said Matt. "I will see that this matter wastes no more of our time."

"Where do he," wondered Wally aloud, "do he's business?"

SEVENTEEN

CITY HALL WAS empty this summer afternoon and the building had the quiet of a school an hour after the closing bell. Matt could go home in the time between the private and public meeting but he decided that he would drive out to a car dealership on Kenmount Road. His Camry was showing age and for reasons, something to do with his decision to run federally, he felt he should be in a Mercedes. Mostly he did not want to return home and express his dismay over Patty's Facebook posts. Maybe, when he told her of his intention to stand for St. John's South, he could suggest she adopt a low profile for the sake of the campaign. No need to bring religion into it, right?

Councillor Cappello emerged from the Planning Department, carting cardboard tubes.

"Councillor Cappello."

"Hello."

"Preparing difficult questions?"

"Getting my facts straight. Kavanagh Court."

"I was...was going to drive out to Bowring Park," Matt said. This wasn't true; Matt had made it up on the spot and now wondered why.

"Concerning Mr. Davenant?"

"Yes." Matt couldn't stop now. "A look, a recce. Facts straight."

"That is probably wise."

"Would you like to come?"

EIGHTEEN

SHE DID. Alessandra wanted to go for a drive with Matt. Needed to. Jules shouldn't be alone for so long she knew. But his sense of time was so disrupted lately she couldn't be sure if he missed her anymore if she was gone for ten minutes or ten hours. He was in a temporal soup gone cold. Sometimes it was plain Jules missed Alessandra even when she was in his company, even as she was holding his hand.

"I suppose I should. We. This situation has to be addressed. Mr. Davenant cannot be left there for too long. Something might...he will come to harm," said Alessandra.

"Harm, yes. It has to be sorted before the fall."

"Fall?"

"Exposure."

"In the press?"

"No, die of exposure. To the elements. Of cold."

"Yes." Alessandra felt inordinately embarrassed she hadn't followed what he'd said, and knew she was blushing.

"Come on," said the mayor.

SHE THOUGHT HE was taking a peculiar route until he pulled into the drive-through of a Tim Hortons on Topsail Road.

"Would you like a coffee?"

"No, thank you."

"I thought Italians were mad for coffee. In the movies they are always stirring their espressos."

He made an affected gesture, pinkie finger out, of turning a spoon around a small cup.

"I love coffee. I'm . . . it's ridiculous, I know, but many Italians are snobs about it."

"Don't go in for the Tim's?" He sounded genuinely surprised.

"No. Don't go in for the Tim's."

"You miss Italy?"

"Yes. Italy really isn't . . . I'm from Venice, which is not really Italy. Well, of course it is, but . . . but yes, lately I do very much miss it. Can I explain? My mother died a year after my father so I was flying back and forth, burying them, sorting the estate. It was all a tangle." Alessandra caught Matt's eye; he was listening. "And the political paralysis of Italia, the embarrassment of the Berlusconi years. Secondary embarrassment, I think they call it." Matt nodded. Alessandra continued. "Place is a museum, you know? Atrophy isn't the word but . . . it is a frustrating place to live. Neither my brother nor I could really afford to stay in the family home; it's rented. After my last trip I think I wanted to forget about Venezia. But recently . . . I don't know why."

"It's home."

"As St. John's is yours."

"Yeah. Home is home."

They were silent for a moment before the mayor said, "What's the opposite of missing something?"

A voice came from the speaker next to the open window.

"Can I take your order please?"

MATT DROVE PAST every entrance to the park known to Alessandra, beyond what she understood to be the gate closest to its western boundary. He drove up a street that traced the park's perimeter to a small gravelled drive canopied by maple and beech. A big Quonset hut nuzzled by trucks and tractors told her this was a service entrance. A sign said that entry was restricted but Matt drove on.

"I'm the mayor," he said, as though he'd heard her thoughts. That being mayor was authority enough was further demonstrated when they were stopped by a worker in overalls striped with blaze-orange tape.

"Oh, Mayor Olford. Off you go. Sorry about that."

"Keep up the good work," Matt said with a wave.

Matt steered them to a stretch of pavement too narrow to have been intended for vehicular traffic and drove, rather too fast, into the park. They passed the public pool, crossed a short overpass, and pulled over on the verge below a wooden pavilion.

"Let's go deer hunting," he said.

THERE WAS NOTHING predatory about their advance. Alessandra saw that Matt seemed content to amble; he wasn't stalking anything.

"What do you suppose is wrong with buddy?" he asked.

"Mr. Davenant? Some sort of delusional state," Alessandra said. "You've heard of Stendhal syndrome?"

"No."

"People becoming disoriented, not knowing who they are, hallucinating, after experiencing great beauty. Happens sometimes to tourists in Venezia, in Venice. In museums it occurs. Something like that."

"It can't be easy, living in the park."

"Maybe it was a greater effort being who he was."

"I don't understand it. Maybe I can't," said Matt.

"Can anyone? Does anyone know what it is to be you? To be Mayor Matt Olford? I'd say it isn't such a struggle. You are an attractive man, and good-looking people have it easy. A big hockey star once. People want to be with you. You can just drive into the park with a wave, 'I'm the mayor.' Life can't be hard for you."

"You're right, people don't know. Do I even know?" said Matt. "That guy, that Purcell guy, he used a word for Deer Man, 'sovereignty'?"

"Yes, I heard that. Apparently Mr. Davenant is certainly exercising... I don't know ... self-rule."

"I guess."

"But then, by extension, suicide is sovereignty."

"You've lost me now, professor."

"I'm a librarian."

"Worse."

They walked for a while in silence.

"I'm not as conservative as you think," Matt said. Alessandra couldn't think why.

"Yes you are," she answered.

"I'm a...I am a fiscal conservative but people can do what they like. I want people to do what they like. I don't want to live somewhere where people feel they can't be who they are, can't say what they like. If Mr. Davenant wants to *be* a deer..."

They'd backtracked to walk under the bridge over which they'd moments ago driven. Three teenage boys were lounging in the shade on the slope of the bank where it met the undercarriage of the overpass. One of them called out.

"Gonna suck him off, missus?"

Matt stopped and sighed. He drew a breath and barked, "Get down here."

"Or is he a faggot?" Their spokesman was a black-haired boy. He was smoking a cigarette.

"It's 'Your Worship, Mayor Faggot' to you," Matt said in a voice Alessandra had never before heard. "Come down and say hello, *Beautiful*."

The boys received something, a man-to-man signal that Alessandra didn't fully grasp, a message worse than Matt's words themselves. They were suddenly afraid of Matt. The three boys commenced crab-walking to the edge of the slope. Reaching daylight they dropped, legs churning to run before they even hit the ground.

"You scared them off."

"I wish I had the knees to chase them. Maybe."

They wandered until they reached a seldom-used path cut into a steep bank paralleling a gorge through which ran the Waterford River. They were shaded, scattered beams of sunlight cut through the leaves above to show off mist rising from the rapids they could hear, but not see, below.

"Sure Davenant doesn't think he's a mountain goat?" asked Matt.

"At night you might..."

"Pitch right over the edge. Yes, easily."

They came to a bench, its etiolated wood turning moss green. Matt sat down and draped his arms the full length of it. Alessandra stood for a moment before him and then, without any sense of having chosen to do so, placed herself on the seat next to him, touching him.

"Councillor Cappello...Alessandra?"

"Yes?"

"I...when I asked you to...We really do have to determine. It is something we have to look at."

"I know. It's an urgent situation. Not an emergency but also...Matt, today I felt, today I—"

His arm pulled her in and up. She craned her neck and dropped back her head to let his mouth meet hers. Her hand pressed to his heart as her lips parted. His left hand cradled her side, overtook the length of her ribs so she felt small. She brought her hand down and felt, right away, heat and muscle.

A panting dog, dripping river, was eyeing them. They could hear its owner's voice and another approaching, two men jabbering. Alessandra went to stand. For a second it seemed as if Matt would not let her go, was holding her down, but his hand fell away and she got to her feet in time to greet them.

"Hello," she said.

NINETEEN

THE MAN WAS in distress. He was standing on a patch of grass, off a concrete walk, on the margin of the supermarket parking lot. He was unsure where to go. He wasn't carrying groceries so Audrey Manning first reasoned he had forgotten or lost his wallet. Then, walking past, she saw that his condition was not one of agitation but confusion. Audrey turned back to help.

"Have you lost your wallet?"

"I shaved and now . . ."

"Yes?" Audrey encouraged, noticing his belt had missed two loops and his trousers were at risk of falling down.

"Where were we?" he said.

"Is everything okay?" she asked.

The man handed Audrey his wallet and said, "I'm not the person on that list."

He was a handsome older man, consumed by fear. He was unshaven. Audrey took the offered wallet and opened it. His driver's licence said his name was Jules Bowan. He lived on

Rennie's Mill Road. The identifying photograph on the laminated card showed a confident figure, unafraid. Audrey wondered for a second if she knew the name, but then she saw so many in her work as the mayor's secretary.

"Maybe you should go home, Mr. Bowan. Do you have a way home?"

Mr. Bowan shook his head.

"Can I give you a drive home? Let me take you home."

MR. BOWAN RELAXED once Audrey coaxed him into her car. It was as if she had driven him home this way hundreds of times before. He seemed to be taking in the sights.

In less than ten minutes Audrey was pulling into the driveway of a lovely home, the address on Jules Bowan's driver's licence. The yard was wild with unkempt rose bushes and annuals in ad hoc beds. As soon as the car stopped Mr. Bowan said, "Thank you so much for the ride."

He opened his door, stepped from the vehicle, and made his way to the house as if everything were fine. Unconvinced, Audrey decided to follow. She was met by a neighbour, a woman in her sixties, in a man's work shirt and thick knee pads. She wore cloth gardening gloves and was holding a trowel.

"Did you…?"

"I found him at Sobeys on Merrymeeting Road. He seemed disoriented."

"He has Alzheimer's."

"Yes, I gathered that was the…"

"Poor creature. I know them. I keep a key." The woman gestured at the house. "Let me…"

"You sure?"

"Yes. Very kind of you to bring him home."

"It was no trouble."

"They are going to have to do something, if he is going to start wandering. Care of some sort." The neighbour lay down her trowel on the stone wall lining the driveway and took off her gloves.

"Yes," said Audrey. "Home care."

"For a time, but..."

"Of course."

"His wife is a young woman. Not *young* young but not... not a senior like Mr. Bowan," said the neighbour.

TWENTY

MATT TOOK THE quickest route back to City Hall, along Waterford Bridge Road. Glancing at the speedometer he caught himself doing sixty-five kilometres an hour in a fifty zone. Reduction of speed on this stretch of road was a cause he'd championed.

"It's not . . ." he said.

"I love Jules. I love my husband," she said.

"I know. It's the same with me, I . . . but that has nothing to do with it."

"I know. It's nothing to do with it," said Alessandra. "I wanted to and I did. I don't feel I should regret, but . . ."

"I know," said Matt. But he felt an utter fool, felt more ashamed and embarrassed than he had in years. He was sorry for what he'd done, but sorry also for himself. He was a fool. He was a fool. He was a fool.

TWENTY-ONE

ALESSANDRA HAD NOT known this sort of shame since she was a child, a weight of dishonour, the sense of all the eyes in the town on you. She was overcome with more than a desire to kiss Matt; it was a demand. It was not her fault and yet she felt blame, felt the admonition of her dead mother. Her mother! And every second sitting next to Matt in his car a howling, a baying of disgrace in her head was amplified. It was a kiss, only a kiss. Was that so wrong? It was nothing to be ashamed of. She took out her phone to check for messages. It was the only way out of this moment.

"Oh hello, Alessandra, it's Kathleen. I'm in your house now. Fixed Jules a cup of tea. A woman brought him home from Sobeys. He was wandering. I'll stay here until you can get home. No worries."

She couldn't ask Matt to take her, not home, she would go to City Hall, get in her own car and go. Putting the phone back in her purse she saw the prescription for Reminyl, a new drug the doctor suggested for Jules, that she had neglected to fill.

"I...I may not make the public meeting tonight," she said.

"Not because of..."

"No, no, something else altogether." They were turning into City Hall. Matt was going to park in the space reserved for the mayor, closest to the front doors, in plain view. "Can you let me out by the garage?"

"Of course," Matt said, stopping the car. "You all right?"

"Yes, Matt, this is...it's nothing to do with...we will have to talk."

"We will."

TWENTY-TWO

"ARE YOU HUNGRY?" Patty called. She heard Matt close the front door behind him.

"Yeah," he answered.

"I waited. Come on, I'm starving."

She'd cooked a ham and mac and cheese. There was a small bowl of salad and about a half a bottle of red wine in the middle of the table. There was a glass of wine at Matt's place setting.

"This is delicious," Matt told her. It was.

"I had all these ends, nubs of different kinds of cheese, so there's like Parmesan, and old cheddar and that expensive French one. Saint-Nectaire?"

"It's great."

"Gourmet mac and cheese, hey?" she said.

"How was your day?" asked Matt.

"Good, good. Do you like this wine?"

"I do."

"From up in Canada." She picked up the bottle and

examined the label. "How was the council meeting?"

"Okay."

"Anything about the Deer Man?"

"No. Why do you ask?"

"I saw a Facebook thing today," she said, thinking the ham did not taste the way ham used to, that there was a chemical tang to the meat that was never there when she was a girl, when it was ringed with white fat and rind and not, as now, uniformly pink and the shape of something extruded. She'd been thinking lately of trying to avoid all processed foods, to be more mindful of what they ate.

"What sort of thing?" Matt asked.

"A page supporting him."

"You support him, Pats?"

"NO! I think it's disgusting. It's a sort of perversion. Can they not . . . help him?"

"What can *they* do? *They* don't even know where the mind resides."

"'Mind' or 'spirit'?"

"People are going to argue that it's his right to be whoever he likes."

Patty thought Matt's tone was condescending.

"Which people?" she said.

"Some people came to a committee meeting and then met me in the office. These . . . there's . . . every sort of 'pride' organization," Matt said. "There's 'mad pride' now. I know there are going to be people coming out of the woodwork saying it's a good thing that he's a deer."

"Pride goeth before a fall."

"Nothing religious please, Pats."

"Becoming an animal, Matt?"

"Hey, I'm not defending it," he said.

"But are you...?"

"He's trespassing," Matt said, "and if he stays out there until the fall he'll die of exposure. It's too foolish for words, really."

"I think it's wrong. I think it's..." Patty shook her head. She thought it was devilish but she wouldn't say. "That's not what's in the Bible anyway, 'Pride goeth before a fall.' It doesn't say that," she said. "It's from Proverbs. It actually goes 'Pride goeth before *destruction*.'"

"Right."

"'...a *haughty spirit* before a fall.'" She watched Matt nod in a way she knew meant he didn't want to hear anymore. He wouldn't come out and say it but he was hostile to anything to do with her church. It wasn't disinterest; it was antagonism. "Gonna have some more mac and cheese, honey?"

"Pats... there is something we have to talk about. Something's happened." Matt lay down his fork and knife. Patty felt as though there was something in her throat.

"What is it, Matthew?"

"I got a call from the Prime Minister's Office."

"The prime minister of Canada?"

"Yes. I was invited to run in St. John's South next election. They've done some polling and it looks like I stand a good chance. More than good probably."

Why did Matt seem so grave?

"That's good news, isn't it?" she said. "Matthew! The prime minister! A tremendous vote of confidence, if anything?"

"Sure," said Matt.

"And?"

"And I think I'm going to do it. It's an interesting time in St. John's but...bigger stage, change too. Get us out of town. With Katie and Jack away at school, what's keeping us here?"

"I think it's a great idea, honey. I do." She had to catch her breath. "Incredibly exciting, Matthew."

"Yes."

"They would put you right in Cabinet, being the only one from Newfoundland. You speak French. Wow. When are you going to—"

"Nothing is public yet. I'll get back to them soon and then... There's a thing, though."

"A thing?'

"We, you and I, are gonna have to watch more closely any...in public...stuff like social media too, Facebook. Keep it boring."

"Of course."

"Religious...don't want to... The media will grab hold of anything."

"I understand," she said.

"Great, thanks."

"Did you know, Matt, that the prime minister is a member of the Christian and Missionary Alliance?"

"Not until the man from the Prime Minister's Office told me, which makes my point."

"Yes, Matt, it does."

TWENTY-THREE

GARY MACKENZIE DID not like Newfoundlanders.

The Toronto Metro Police said they would relocate Gary anywhere in Canada. Newfoundland was booming, a touch exotic, and reputedly "friendly" at a time when Gary needed companionship. New friends in a newfound land, why not?

But on arrival Gary found the people nosy, clannish, and inordinately pleased with themselves. They looked inward and uncritically loved all they observed; the views the fish the berries the mountains the music. A native daughter working in the Los Angeles porn industry had recently set a record for copulating with the most partners in a day and so was a local hero. The mayor of the capital city once played a few shifts in the NHL and they carried on like he was Bobby Orr.

They were too talkative and overly familiar. Female shop clerks called him "dear" or "my love" and even "my lover." A secretary back at the cop shop, Joanne, a married woman in her fifties, never failed to put her hand on his back when talking with him. But if you were not born to them you were never going to be of them. They weren't countrymen; they were a sprawling family nine generations from their shipwreck.

Gary sent an email to his Toronto task force case officer last week reporting that the move to Newfoundland was a failure and that he wished to go elsewhere. Gary did not mention that he was worried that someone in St. John's, an animal rights activist, might have recognized him.

He'd expected, despite never having been promised, to be living in the downtown of St. John's, in some candy-coloured Victorian house like those he'd seen on television commercials. That variety of housing was in short supply and, once converted from rooming-house tenements, costly. The condos in the city centre were no different than any in North America, squat and poorly built, so Gary ended up in a subdivision called Southlands, which could have been a suburban tract in Etobicoke but for the wind and the wet.

More concerning, he reported, was that any pretense of discretion regarding the circumstances of his relocation seemed to have been abandoned before his arrival. Every cop in the Royal Newfoundland Constabulary knew his story, or a part of it. The fellow cop sitting next to him in the front seat of the cruiser, Constable Kevin Maher, was now plumbing Gary for details.

"So your fake name was a dead feller's?" Kev was from some rural quarter of the island, one of its innumerable bays, and retained his accent. The ways of speaking here were too many and various to sort out and all equally cranky to Gary's ear.

"Died in infancy, parents moved to England soon after."

"And 'e a Gary too. That was good fortune, make it easier for you to pretend."

"They look for that. When they are making the legend they look for someone with the same first name."

Kev considered this. "Like you would."

Having come up from two full years undercover, underground, *living* as a subversive, Gary expected assignments reflecting his skills, serious investigative work, but the locals kept the big cases for themselves. There was a double homicide in Shaheen's Trailer Park yesterday—a pond of blood and viscera, according to reports, teeth all over the place—that should have been his, but Chief Cahill, to whom Gary complained about not getting the assignment, said Gary needed to better learn the lay of the land before taking on such a high-profile matter. The press would be "all over you," the chief said. Gary was promised a pending high-stakes fraud case, but he was never going to meet women that way. It was the big murders and rapes, the violence that enthralled the gals, that made you as interesting as the latest serial killer on the tube. No, instead of chasing down a two-time murderer, Gary was sitting, in a fine new suit, in a cruiser rank with man stink, in a city park on the lookout for some nutcase who had allegedly taken up residence in the bushes. Rather than asking the questions, Gary was answering them, and his interrogator was a hick who looked sixteen years old.

"And the crowd you were investigating dey were...like, 'terrorists'?"

"No, they were anti-globalization activists. Some of them were anarchists," said Gary.

"Dey were going to make away with the world leaders?"

"They were going to disrupt the G20. How, we didn't know. I'm not comfortable talking about it. I'm not supposed to."

"Reads ya. I don't think we got any anarchists here in Newfoundland. Dere's dem that don't believe in the law, your regular robber, right." Kev considered the question more deeply. "And I allows dere's dem don't even know dere is a 'system.'"

They sat for a while in silence, listening to static and chatter on the radio. Hold up at the Marie's Minimart on Topsail Road, a teenage girl missing from Shea Heights, domestic disturbance in Quidi Vidi.

"Buddy thinks 'e's a deer," said Kev.

"Yeah," said Gary.

"You believes dat?"

"Sure," said Gary, adding, "there's no 'normal,' Kev."

"No?"

"No, 'normal' is the stupidest idea ever. There's no such thing."

"I don't know, b'y."

"Year ago, in Toronto, in Rosedale, which is a well-to-do 'hood," said Gary, "I answered a call, a 10-97. A guy was dead at the bottom of a flight of stairs with his dick in his hand. Turns out he's like one of the best oboe players in the world, tours all over the place. Hong Kong one night, Berlin the next. Classical music, right. Thing about it was, he could only get sexually aroused when he was falling down stairs. He'd broken almost every bone in his body over the years. This night, which he must have seen coming, it was a bone in his neck. He couldn't have chosen that. It was who he was. Maybe this guy *is* a deer."

"But police work, inspector," Kev said, "is kind of about 'normal.'"

"I suppose that's true, Kev."

Kev grasped the steering wheel, pulling himself forward, bringing his face closer to the windshield.

"Luh," he said.

Gary looked in the same direction as Kev. A gap in the trees on the other side of a mowed field indicated a path, but Gary saw no activity.

"See 'e?" asked Kev. It took Gary a moment to understand.

"No. I don't see anybody."

"See the trail?"

"Yes."

"Two o'clock."

Gary still could see nothing beyond branches and leaves and light and shade.

"You sure?"

"I sees 'e," said Kev, opening his door and stepping from the car without making a sound. Gary again tried to trace the line from Kev's unwavering gaze to movement or a flash of colour at the tree line, but he was blind to whatever was there.

"Don't imagine he can hear us all the way over there, Constable Maher."

"Shhhh...sir." Kev gestured that he was going to proceed west and then come up north to the spot and that Gary should loop around the other way. Gary must have looked unconvinced, for Kev gave him a reassuring smile and one of those Newfie flicks of the head before capering off, bent and low to the ground. After a moment Gary got out and did as he was told by his subordinate. There was no way he was going to mess up the suit by crashing around in the woods, he thought.

TWENTY-FOUR

REDUCED TO BEGGING for gigs and no one had even shown Lloyd the courtesy of returning a call. Looking at his inbox Lloyd saw his email entreaties were similarly unanswered. His latest futile petition was to a hack he knew back in Los Angeles named Elliot Jonson, improbably now head-in-chief at the CBC in Toronto. Was Lloyd such a pariah he couldn't even get a meeting at the lowly CBC? Yes, he was toxic. There was no loyalty in showbiz. You couldn't count on anyone in the racket.

Gin was reliable. Gin you could count on. Even Tanqueray stood up when there wasn't Plymouth to be had.

He sipped an eponymous Donnelly, the tumbler slippery and wanting to slide from his hand. Three measures of gin, one of Lillet, one of soda, and lime over ice. Proper ice, nice fat cubes. Last Lloyd heard, the cocktail's inventor, Dapper Donnelly, was in the constant company of tax lawyers. Poor bastard. Donnelly was the best sort of man with whom to booze but a disastrous financial adviser. Lloyd's networks were becoming patchwork.

He willed a reverie; a couple, three Donnellys and a few rails of the best blow, under the pergola in the garden of his place in the Hills. Those were the days when Lloyd could afford to be the one not returning calls. Knowing he was only now getting what he deserved didn't make it any better. It made it worse.

Lloyd had come to dread opening the laptop on his brother's dining table. No return emails from anyone in show business but ever increasing traffic on Harry Davenant's Facebook page.

Jaysus H. Christ some local artiste was trying to document Harry's "journey" in photographs, because Mr. Davenant's was "an important story that needs to be told," but he couldn't get close enough for a clear snap and was wondering if Harry responded to any "calls." Yes, thought Lloyd, but only from his agent. Gin.

There was a message Natalie had forwarded from some prof at the university who was writing a paper in which she was "asking again the unanswered 'Question of the Animal.'" Lloyd scanned the long note — "animal theory," "Felix Guattari," "being naked," "the doggishness of Diogenes." She was asking permission for what? And from whom, exactly? There was no better place for a lunatic to hide in plain sight than the Academy. Gin.

Why had Lloyd done it? Why had he planted the mischievous fib, put in their ears the lie that Harry was a deer? Storytelling for its own sake, a blue-balled hack's wank? To prove how easily led was the crowd?

Bitterness broke only its bearer. Whose fault was it that the LSPU Theatre closed down ten days before Lloyd's play was going to open? Not Harry's. Lloyd never expected the deer story would have such legs and it was still vaulting fences. Gin. Gin.

If only Harry had not said to Lloyd that he was as happy, "happier even," working with Sentry as a security guard. "Happier even"! That was what poisoned Lloyd. That was what made him do it. Not Harry's sentiment, but that it could be true, that he could be happier as a security guard.

Lloyd got up from the table and went to the door in the kitchen that exited into the backyard, deciding he should, with his brother Dave soon returning from France, accede to the demand that he not smoke in the house.

He'd stopped into Caines Grocery the day before, to pick up the deck of fags, and they'd changed the whole place, renovated and modernized and modularized the works.

Where would Lloyd go when Dave got back? What would he do? What would he do?

TWENTY-FIVE

General Occurrence Report

Case Heading:
Date Reported to Police: 2013/07/02   **Time:** 15:30
Earliest Date Occurred: 2013/06/20   **Time:** unknown
Drugs/Alcohol Consumed: Yes   **No** X
Location of Occurrence: Bowring Park, St. John's
Location of Incident: Open area/public park
Occupied by: Accused only
Weapon Type: N/A
Vehicle Type: N/A
Shoplifting: N/A
Stolen Property: N/A
Type of Fraud: N/A
Motor Vehicle Recovery:
CCJS: Accused committed to mental hospital
Complainant notified upon conclusion of file: Yes 2013/07/12

How Notified: By phone

Submitted by: Inspector Gary Mackenzie 2013/07/13 Awaiting disposition

Accused, Harry Davenant of 72 Cochrane Street, was reported present in Bowring Park after closing. Multiple reports that accused was sleeping in the park. Other unsubstantiated reports that accused is suffering delusion of being an animal. Accused was hiding in wooded areas and avoiding contact. Park official reported surprising accused on trail in rarely visited part of the park and shouting at him as he ran away that accused could not be in the park at night. On 2013/07/09 Constable Markham told accused to leave park as accused successfully broke away from a foot pursuit in heavy brush.

On 2013/07/11 at approximately 17:30 accused was spotted hiding in wooded area by Constable Kevin Maher. Constable Maher and Inspector Mackenzie pursued the accused. After lengthy foot chase Constable Maher apprehended the accused. Accused was cooperative but uncommunicative. Decision was made to take accused to psychiatric emergency where attending physician suggested accused be held for observation.

TWENTY-SIX

ALESSANDRA ONCE HEARD the term *muscle memory* and wondered if Jules seeming at ease, in his chair with a book in his
hands, looking for all the world like he was reading, was an
example. Did he remember *how* to be when he could no longer
recall the *what* of things? Alessandra monitored his progress
through the volume of Goldoni he was holding and determined
he wasn't following any logical course. It was a book from their
case that a scholar with a focus on things Venetian should
know but which Jules, to this point, thought Alessandra, had
never before opened. She couldn't be sure if he hadn't picked
a volume at random. She judged he was on the same page for
days. He was going through the motions, and they were rock-
ing him like a baby. Perhaps she shouldn't interrupt him, leave
well enough alone.

"Jules?"

"Yes."

"What happened today? Did you get lost?"

"They've changed it all."

"Yes, they have. Do you feel…do we need to get someone to help you when I'm not here?"

"It's that they changed it all around. If I'm familiar with the situation I will be fine," Jules said. "I got confused because they changed it all around."

"What did you want at the supermarket?"

"Sooner not say." Jules looked as if he wished to return to his book.

"Okay," said Alessandra. "Did you take that new medicine?"

"I took my medication. It made me dopey. I don't want to fall asleep and forget something. What I do, so I won't forget I've put the kettle on, is I put on the timer every time I put on the stove."

"That is a good idea."

"What did you get up to today? Were you at the university?" asked Jules, sounding entirely like his former self. Such echoes were now so rare as to be jarring.

"I went to Bowring Park to look for the man who thinks he's a deer."

"Venison."

"I hope not." Alessandra laughed. "Though I suppose if there is someone crazy enough to imagine they are a deer there is someone else crazy enough to hunt them."

"Venison. Venice. The Veneti…that word…it's, that word is from a Proto-Indo-European root, *μen*—to want, to desire, to love."

"I didn't know," said Alessandra.

"Related to *venus*, of course, love, and Sanskrit *vanas*, which is lust. *Venal* must be. And to the Germanic *wini* and the Old English *wine*, which means *friend*." Jules smiled.

TWENTY-SEVEN

HOW HAD MS. STOKES, the social worker at the mental hospital, found Natalie? Through social media, Lloyd supposed. Good place for a social worker, social media. In each case, Lloyd judged the usage of *social* fuzzy, but then so were the times. Lloyd thought, every day now, that he should give up the fight, accept that the language war was over and lost and simply start texting every banal thought that came into his head in SMS chat abbreviations. Time for Lloyd to lay down arms, or better, don the uniform of one of the enemy's fallen. "LOFL. JS"

There was a poster encouraging safe sexual practices on the wall of the interview room. Why not? Head cases fucked as often as anyone, no? More, probably.

How old was this Ms. Stokes? Late twenties? Early thirties or late? Natalie's vintage, the age until recently he could forget he was not.

"No," she was saying to Natalie. No?

"No," Ms. Stokes said, "we should be clear about this. Mr.

Davenant is not being released to your care."

"Oh," said Natalie, "I thought..."

"I couldn't locate any family. And the examining psychiatrist says he's not suffering any delusions."

"I'm glad for that," Natalie said. "That's the argument we've made all along. It's not a delusion. Can we have a copy of the report?"

"I'm not sure why..."

"It would bolster our case."

"His medical record is private."

"Of course." Lloyd thought it a wise time to jump in. "And as so little else is these days. What's the story with the police?"

"They aren't going to arrest him. But if he returns to the park they will have no choice. They'll probably charge him with trespassing and the park administration will likely get a peace bond."

"Of course," said Lloyd again.

"I'll go get him," said Ms. Stokes. "He can keep the clothes." She left the room without shutting the door.

"I have to say I'm pleasantly surprised," said Natalie. "The psychiatric community are never so progressive. They're agents for Big Pharma."

"I have no doubt you're right," said Lloyd, thinking he'd drop something from Big Pharma now if he had it. He noticed for the first time how odd was Natalie's dress. An oversized baby-blue thick wool sweater fell over and exposed one of her shoulders. The top covered yet exaggerated her bum. She was wearing tights checkered with repeated Warhol images of Elvis. On her feet were high-top, bright burgundy, heavily-heeled Doc

Martens. She didn't need the extra height. "Harry will at least appreciate the lift home."

"I guess one doesn't have any sort of gathering," Natalie said.

"I don't follow."

"When released from a mental institution."

"Like a party?"

"A small one," Natalie said.

"No, I don't think so, not traditionally."

Over Natalie's bare shoulder Lloyd saw him. "Here he comes."

"Act natural," Natalie said.

"Ah, Harry," he said.

Harry went to a wall, putting his back against it. Lloyd thought Harry's posture was never so proper.

"Harry!!!" Natalie went to hug the friend for whom she advocated without having ever met but saw that his position, flat against the wall, prevented his being embraced. "Don't you look wonderful."

She was right. Harry was deeply tanned, bronzed as a yachtsman and almost lean. He must have dropped thirty pounds. He was in clothes quite unlike any Lloyd had known him to wear, beige cargo pants, a long-sleeved light turquoise T-shirt featuring some kind of product logo — a grinning purple fruit or berry — and white canvas deck shoes. He looked past Natalie, ignored her, and, unsmiling, found Lloyd's eye.

Lloyd knew actors, knew the maddest methods, knew the cool-headed psychopaths who could happily inhabit a soul built by a scribbler because they didn't possess one of their own.

Lloyd knew lazy fakes who could trade, for the length of a career, on charm. He knew fat-funnies and he knew players so inhumanly beautiful that they had only to stand before the camera to rule it. But he also knew a few of those true artists who governed their parts, who commanded them from within, yes, but also from without, who were in character and outside it, on and up above the stage and silently behind every person in every seat in the house.

What was that look Harry was giving him? *"It was you? Yes, of course. Today I learned it was you. A deer. It had to be you, Lloyd."* Or was Harry pulling some perverse kind of actors' revenge on writers? *"You want me to play a part? I'll play it."*

"Are there any papers, a release, to sign?" Lloyd asked Ms. Stokes, if only to free himself from Harry's menacing regard.

"No. Mr. Davenant is free to go."

Lloyd looked back and still Harry's eyes were on him. "Then, shall we?" Lloyd said.

Harry got ahead of Lloyd and Natalie in the hallways of the hospital. It didn't seem as if his gait was any quicker but he was better able to glide through the crowd, find the gaps.

An old woman stinking of piss howled a goodbye at the door. Harry was down the stone steps and on his way to the parking lot. Had he seen where Natalie parked her vehicle from a window within the institution?

"Harry? Harry, we're..."

She was unheard. Harry broke into a weightless lope, like a lifelong runner starting his kilometres but with a higher, almost balletic kick. In less than six strides he cleared the parking lot. He bounded across the road without checking for traffic and, as quick as that, put the green of a loose hedge behind him and was gone.

Lloyd felt Natalie's hand in his, squeezing it. She was dew-eyed, her lip quivering at what they had witnessed. It was as if they were seeing their child off to his first day of kindergarten.

TWENTY-EIGHT

MATT SENSED THAT Alessandra needed to talk about what happened between them as urgently as he did. But fate denied them. As the last Parks and Public Spaces Committee concluded it seemed as if they might steal a moment when Planning Durnford intruded with another of his epic complaints. Alessandra simply walked away.

Now, in the Monday private meeting of council, Matt was, from his elevated position at the front of the chamber, trying to catch her eye and communicate that they should stay behind when it was over. His efforts were impeded by Alessandra's preoccupation with explaining something to Wally O'Neill that Matt knew Wally could never comprehend.

"Parking garages work against density; we are trying to *increase* density," she said.

"Can't put anyt'ing up. Can't build anyt'ing."

"No, Councillor O'Neill, you are not listening. I want to vote to *approve* the development. The proponent could have invested more in a structure of at least some architectural interest, but I agree the office space is needed." Alessandra's speech slowed now, as if she was explaining something to a young child. "I want the proposed parking garage severed from the proposal for the office building because I want to vote against the parking garage."

Matt watched Alessandra sit. She touched the tips of the fingers on her right hand to her temple as if to stem budding pain.

"See, dat's foolish," said Wally. "Dey has to have a place to park."

"NOT IF THEY DON'T HAVE CARS!" Alessandra said without rising.

"Councillor Cappello, you see the rent this crowd will be charging? Their tenants will have cars," said Councillor Neary.

"*Of course* they will own cars, but they will go to work without them."

"Why would dey do dat?" said Wally.

"Because there would be nowhere to park them."

"You've lost me now, missus." Wally laughed and, glancing toward Councillor Jardine, pointed at Alessandra as if to say, "Look at 'er, luh!"

Matt sensed Alessandra was about to say something she would regret, so he interjected.

"What she is saying, Wally, is that we want fewer cars coming downtown. Surely you see that the roads are blocked with traffic."

"Half a dat is people driving around in circles looking for a parking spot," said Wally.

"Around 10 percent of traffic," said Planning Durnford, "at

any time, is searching for a parking spot."

"What a horrible thought," said Alessandra.

"And while the roads"—Matt saw Wally was distracted and repeated himself—"while the roads, Wally, are at capacity, public transit is not. People won't use transit because they should but because it makes life easier."

"Having more cars than parking spaces isn't making my life easier." Wally sounded smug, as if he knew, really knew, that he was winning the argument. "Your Worship."

"So can we please," said Matt, "have the proposal redrafted? Make two separate applications—one for the office building and another for the parking garage."

The trio of staff attending the meeting nodded in such a way as to show their displeasure at having more to do.

"You votin' for or against the garage, Your Worship?" asked Wally.

"I haven't made up my mind but I think I'm leaning toward Councillor Cappello's view."

Wally looked surprised.

"You stipulate parking minimums in a town, Wally. Whether we like it or not this is becoming more and more a city, and I think that means moving to stipulated parking maximums."

"Wha?"

"We put conditions on new development, saying they can only have a maximum number of parking spaces."

Wally stared at Matt for a moment and then shook his head, pitying Matt's lack of understanding.

"Next," said Matt.

Councillor Mercer stood.

"I know you haven't had much time to look at the documents I've tabled but I thought, why make such good news wait?"

The chamber filled with the sound of those within shuffling through papers.

"We have a sponsor for the park at Kavanagh Court. Jerome Bridger of Botwood Beverages has agreed to . . ."

Scanning the papers in his hands, Matt saw who this was. So did Wally, who exclaimed "Jerry Juice!"

"The same," said Councillor Mercer. "Mr. Bridger will pay the shot, naming privileges on the park, of course, and the Jerjuice logo on some of the interpretation stations and any signage."

"Jerjuice?" Alessandra was not putting it together. "Is? Forgive my ignorance. It is . . . ?"

"It's a sports drink," Wally enthused.

"I don't think," Matt said, "that he is allowed to call Jerjuice a 'sports drink' anymore."

"Newfoundland berries all the same," said Mercer.

"Entrepreneur," said Wally. "Great Newfoundland entrepreneur."

"Not allowed?" wondered Alessandra, still surveying the document.

"The juices are caffeinated and sweetened so . . ." said Matt.

"Delicious juice," said Wally. "Youngsters loves it."

"A great Newfoundland product and brand," said Matt, "no doubt about it. A rare and welcome success."

"And the park at Kavanagh Court will be" — Alessandra

checked the document— "Bridger Park?"

"Jerjuice Park, I believe," said Mercer.

Matt watched Alessandra cover her face with her hands.

"These are our times," said Matt, speaking only to Alessandra.

"What is the logo?" asked Alessandra.

"It's like a big blueberry," said Mercer. "It should have been included in the proposal I s'pose. Big Blueberry head. Like Jerry's face, only on a blueberry."

"Das it," said Wally.

"Interpretation and signage?" asked Alessandra.

"You know," said Mercer, "signs explaining what the various plants in the park are, Play Safe, Pick Up after Your Pooch, that sort of thing."

"I'm against interpretation," said Alessandra. "It limits experience."

"Wha?" said Wally.

"I'm not getting into it," Alessandra said as she stood, gathered up her papers from her desk, and left the room.

TWENTY-NINE

NATALIE HAD LIVED alone so long it felt strange to have a man in the house. A gentleman caller. Lloyd was a gentleman too, well-spoken, worldly. He wasn't what she would call handsome; there was something worn about him and he'd lost his hair. She preferred a man with a full head of hair. Much preferred hair.

When Natalie's divorce from Derek was final, a year ago, she resolved to make new male friends. She would not become one of those bitter, man-hating, middle-aged exes. And her brief dalliance with the same sex and life in Vancouver was a disaster she wanted to never again recall. Actually, thinking about it, her divorce from Derek was finalized more than two years ago. Almost three. Derek's hair was extravagant, thicker than even her own.

"It's an Australian shiraz," she said, handing Lloyd a glass of wine.

"Lovely," he said.

"I guess you know all about Californian wine, having lived there."

"Not really," he said. "My brother is the wine snob. He could tell you all about it—grape varieties, different vineyards, the role of microbiology in *terroir*—bore you to tears. For me it comes down to red or white."

"My brother Andrew too, he's a tremendous wine snob. Has, like, this enormous temperature-controlled cellar under his house in Rosedale. He doesn't drink them as far I can tell. Looks at the labels and shows them off. You don't mind lentil walnut loaf?"

"Sounds perfectly delicious."

"If I'd known you were coming I would have made maybe a mushroom risotto. That's something meat eaters like too."

"And a nice old bottle of Barbaresco," said Lloyd.

"That's a sort of wine?"

"Yes. From northern Italy."

"I've felt so much better since I went completely vegan," Natalie said. "And not only physically—it has really cleared my head."

"Then it's a good thing I'm eating it because my head desperately needs clearing."

"I'm sure that's not true. You seem...I don't know...you're so quick, Lloyd. You know what to say right away."

"I work with words...or used to...so it appears that I'm sharper than I am. There's a trick to it," Lloyd said, rising from the couch. What was he doing, Natalie wondered. He went to the mantelpiece and picked up the picture of her and her family, that one in Georgian Bay. "These your kin?"

"All but my oldest brother Walter. He was overseas. We . . . the family kept offices in London. The family business."

"It's like . . . would you call this a lodge?"

"Cottage."

"It's . . . the deck alone . . . the woodwork is exquisite."

"We called it 'the cottage.' The original my grandfather built on the lake was much smaller. Rustic."

"My family had a cabin out Gander Bay way. Nothing more than a shack. Called it 'the shack.' We used to go up there trouting, my brother, my father, and I. I don't even know what became of the place."

"You should go again sometime, see how it matches up with your memories."

"Yes. Yes, I should. You ever go back to Georgian Bay?" Lloyd said, waving the photo.

"Rarely. I'd have to co-ordinate it with my siblings. It's too complicated. I'm the baby of the family and you know how that goes, my brothers and sisters never take me seriously. And they are all, you know, Toronto establishment types. "

Lloyd nodded.

"Go ahead make your Trustafarian comment," she said.

"What? No."

"I can't ever say this because it always comes off all wrong, but . . . well . . . there is a terrible price for being born into wealth."

"I don't doubt it. I was never in so much trouble as when I was flush."

"It's difficult to find your path in life when you don't have to work. Do you get along with your brother?" she asked, wanting to talk about something other than her own family.

"I do."

The timer on the stove sounded.

"Why don't you sit down," she said.

THIRTY

THE LENTIL DISH was flavourful but in want of moisture, sauce. Lloyd wished there was something less cloying than the Australian wine with which to wash it down. A whiskey to go with his after-supper coffee would be nice but he couldn't ask. The coffee, from a stovetop espresso maker, was pleasing. Natalie came from the kitchen with her cup, some sort of herbal tea that smelled like soap and latex.

Lloyd was seated, as before the meal, on the far end of the couch, pitched up against the arm. Before dinner Natalie sat on a chair opposite, pulled into the middle of the room to be closer. Now she sat on the couch, next to Lloyd.

"I feel good about what happened today, with Harry," she said, trying, he saw, to look into his eyes.

"I didn't know what to expect... but still, I didn't expect that," said Lloyd.

"The problem now is going to be keeping well-wishers or the curious away. They would only alert the authorities that

Harry has returned to the park. Would it be ethical of us to tell people he wasn't there?"

"Tell them how?"

"Post something on Facebook. Say he'd ... I don't know ...migrated! You know, down the Southern Shore or something. Are there rules about being truthful on Facebook, I mean laws?"

"I've no idea about Facebook. And the Southern Shore is up not down. Labrador is down."

Natalie looked confused. "How can that be?"

"It's to do with sailing," said Lloyd, wishing he'd not brought it up — or down. "And if Harry ever did go up the Shore he'd be found in someone's freezer, without tags."

"I'm proud of you, Lloyd, proud that you are such a good friend to Harry, that you care so much."

"It nothing more than—"

She was kissing him. She had flung her arms around his neck and pushed her lips to his. Her tongue was in his mouth and he reflexively met it with his own. He pulled her tight and she hoisted a leg, awkwardly, across his lap, kneeing, with a bass thud, the arm of the couch. Now her hands, both big mitts, were over his ears and he felt, briefly, like he was at the bottom of a swimming pool. He brought his hand up to search for her breast, finding it heavier, more substantial, than expected. She was almost a giant.

"Oh, Lloyd."

He shimmied toward the centre of the couch to give her the room to get on top of him but she was heading in the same direction in order to lie down on her back.

"Oh, Lloyd, sorry, watch out."

He pulled back to make space. Natalie let herself drop backwards, swinging her arms up to put them behind her head, and in doing so caught his chin with her elbow. Lloyd's teeth came together with enough vigour to dislodge a sheet of something in his sinuses.

"Sorry," she said.

"Let's go to your bed, Natalie."

"Okay. Yes."

"I'm . . . out of practice," he said.

"I've never had much," she said.

"You were married."

"Even so."

"Like riding a bike," he said.

"Feels like being on a bike?" she said.

"I meant you never forget how," he said.

"I broke my arm learning to ride a bike," she said.

Lloyd took her hand and pulled her up.

"Lloyd, there is one thing I can't . . . it's not that . . . but there is one thing I can't do, in bed, where I'm so strictly vegan, the animal protein, you understand . . ."

THIRTY-ONE

SHE WAS RELIEVED Lloyd was taking charge. She'd made the first move believing she wanted to be the assertive one, the guide, but now, she thought, that leading role would be in some other aspect of their evolving relationship.

He was too old for her. How old was he? Was Lloyd fifty? She wasn't yet thirty-five. She could not do this.

They were scarcely across the threshold of her bedroom when he was out of his shirt. She thought that in every other instance of lovemaking, hitherto in her life, the man had taken off her shirt first and left the undoing of his buttons until she was standing naked before him.

Was it because he was bald she'd imagined him hairless? In the faint light she saw his wide chest was covered in a pelt. There was something of the beast about him, of a boar or a bear. Her flush was becoming febrile. She felt something purr. No longer the gentleman, Lloyd put her roughly on the bed. He pounced on and pinned her. No, it was wolf! Her fingers splayed as wide as they could and she could still not measure his back. He seemed bigger now, out of his clothes, and heavy. He was too old for her, but Natalie liked a big man.

THIRTY-TWO

SOON AFTER PUBERTY, in a single moment of a junior high school history class, seeing and appreciating, for the first time, Carolyn Bungay's voluptuousness, exactly as Gavrilo Princip put a bullet in Archduke Franz Ferdinard of Austria, Lloyd's sexual urges emerged in full. All the lights came on at once, an entire arena was illuminated by the wattage. Now, all these years later, they'd barely dimmed. He'd assumed, wished even, they would fade with age but it hadn't happened, even with the cobalt glow of mortality staining his horizon. The faintest touch and Lloyd was on bust.

Natalie had seemed reticent as they stood by the bed but was now meeting his every thrust with drenched abandon. Noises, gurgles, growls were coming from her; she was clawing at him and now clicking like...like what? It was like a cat stalking a bird! Jaysus, she was snarling and, pulling herself up by his shoulders, making to bite his face.

He knew this, he knew she was mad—all the signs were

there. What was he doing? She howled and snapped again, never ceasing her pelvic reaching. He withdrew, took her by the calves and flipped her over on to her belly; he grabbed her hips and hauled her up to where he could take her from behind. There was something, marks, not symbols or text but a picture or even a map, running between the deep twinned dimples that marked the line where her backside began to bloom. It was a tattoo. Natalie was shaking and quaking at his pounding and Lloyd couldn't make it out. Was it a caterpillar? It was ribbed, laddered, darker at one end, pointed at the other? Was it a feather? Yes, it was feather. It was a tattoo of an eagle feather.

THIRTY-THREE

IT WAS "EUGENE"; Eugene, smiling at Inspector Gary Mackenzie, now of the Royal Newfoundland Constabulary, Eugene standing and waiting for Gary next to the shelves of canned vegetables. Peas and carrots. Corn on the cob in tins, something Gary had never seen before moving to Newfoundland. Eugene no-last-name-given, his "liaison" from the Canadian Security Intelligence Service during the G20 operation in Toronto was waiting, unannounced, for Gary, in an aisle of the Sobeys supermarket on Ropewalk Lane.

Eugene looked into Gary's cart at 1% milk, three lamb chops, a mesh bag of onions, a red pepper, and some forlorn lettuce.

"Eating healthy, Inspector Mackenzie."

"This is not a coincidence."

"I'm here about your letter. No one wants to talk about this stuff on the phone."

"Really?"

"Calls are secure but there would be a record of the call itself."

"Of course."

"Keep shopping," Eugene instructed. He was nondescript, wore a navy blue windbreaker, tan slacks, Clark slip-ons with thick soles. Thinning hair, in an unfortunate cut, same British brown of his shoes, livid bags under eyes set too far apart, half an inch under six feet. Not unfuckable but forgettable.

"I'm sorry, you know," Gary said, pushing his cart on.

"About choosing to move to Newfoundland? You should be sorry. Back-of-beyond. Don't know why you insisted. These problems, the security breaches, it's almost inevitable in a place like this. People have nothing to talk about so they find stuff."

"No, not about that, about... about, back at the G20, not identifying any of the anarchist leadership, just nabbing the small fry."

Eugene waved off Gary's concern.

"Anarchist leadership... it's fluid, right? It's a grey area. Otherwise the staging was a complete success. Much was learned. Systems were tested and, for the most part, responded well. And a lot of valuable relationships were established. Despite some uniforms cracking heads, in the context of policing and crowd management in Toronto, it was a positive outcome. People got what they paid for."

Gary thought he had heard something like a suspect's rehearsed alibi in Eugene's words.

"I'm glad. I never really knew... the larger picture," Gary said.

"You want ketchup?" Eugene was holding up a large soft plastic bottle of the store brand.

"I'm good."

"Ever eat ketchup sandwiches when you were a kid?"

"Yes."

"Me too. Loved them." Eugene put the bottle back, precisely from where he'd taken it. "So, you wanna move house?"

"I understand if it's a problem."

"I didn't fly down here to Newfie to refuse the request."

"What are my options?"

"We have only one."

"It is?"

"Ever heard of the company Dalton Monitor?"

"No."

"They ran a lot of the G20 operation. Consulting. They know all about your work."

"Consulting?"

"The details are boring. It was a private-public partnership. Dalton Monitor has a corporate campus in Embustero, Arizona. Do you know Arizona at all?"

"Not really, no."

"It's in Pima County, nice town, twenty minutes from Tucson. Lotta missile silos down that way. People know not to ask about your work."

"What would I do?"

"They give courses and clinics for law enforcement and security: interrogation methods, surveillance, undercover techniques, private and public again."

"For the good guys?"

"For the family friends. Mostly." Eugene smiled at a wide-eyed boy, riding in the basket seat at the back of a shopping cart pushed past them. "They're prepared to offer you something as a sort of teaching assistant leading to a position as an instructor of some kind. It would be a step up in compensation and they are offering an attractive relocation package."

"How did this—"

"They know the sacrifice you made at the G20 and in moving to Newfoundland and they are grateful."

"I'll take it."

"No. Think it over. Because this is it. After this you are on your own."

"I know already. I can't get out of here fast enough."

"I'll contact you in two weeks for your answer. Keep it in confidence. Don't tell the local police force about it; we'll do that. One day you won't show up for your shift and that'll be it."

"Okay."

"This is nothing to do with your cover being blown?"

"What? No."

"'Cause you called Metro Toronto Police about someone, Sommerville?"

"No, that was... She didn't recognize me. No."

"You are sure?"

"Absolutely. Hundred percent."

"You should have contacted us, Gary. Really."

Gary turned his cart up the next aisle: bottled fluids, pop, and various sorts of "water," but Eugene kept straight on, a satellite leaving orbit, and was out of Gary's sight in a second.

Gary caught up to the cart with the boy in the back and,

stopping, reached high to retrieve a bottle of cheap, no-name sparkling water.

"Carefol," said the boy to Gary. "Bweakable."

THIRTY-FOUR

LLOYD AND DONNELLY were in Donnelly's absurd 1970 Buick
Electra convertible, Donnelly at the wheel, the radio tuned,
as always, to KBUE, early in the morning so the Los Angeles
traffic was uncomplicated, the air though which they pushed
was already ardent. Lloyd sensed they were going to make it,
they'd gotten away clean, when the car's speakers lost their
grip on the music and started crying like sirens. Lloyd fumbled
with the knobs, trying to find a station and keep them safe but
across the dial it was all the sound of panic. No.

No, he was in a bed, the orientation of which he could not
apprehend.

No. He was waking now. This was Natalie's bed, in which
he'd spent the night. These were her fine cotton sheets. The
Mexican music was coming from a speaker in a room downstairs, from the kitchen. Closer was the hiss and toy drum-
ming of a running shower. Pipes were ticking in the walls.
He opened his eyes.

He was not in Los Angeles, not in California, not in the thirty-first state in the Union. He was in St. John's, Newfoundland, Canada's final province. Canada, thought Lloyd, where Gregor Samsa would wake from such uneasy dreams to find himself transformed into a gigantic Timbit.

There were three bottles of prescription meds, a puffer, and a tower of books on the night table.

The Radiant Fruit: Veganism and Your Yi'cha 加字

Pharadora IV: Awakens the Fire Dragon

Harry Potter and the Prisoner of Azkaban

Loving More

VacciNation

The Metro Dogs of Moscow

Mounted by the Gryphon

Ravished by the Triceratops

Lloyd sat up. He reached for the volume on the top of the stack. On the back cover there was a bold-faced warning.

"Warning: This is a tale of monster sex. This story was written to unlock your darkest fantasies and innermost desires. It is not for the faint of heart and is not your mother's erotica. All of the sexual descriptions found in this book are very explicit in nature. It's not suitable for someone under eighteen years of age. Read at your own risk."

So dino-porn was now *a thing*. When did Lloyd stop moving forward with the culture, when did he pull over and, without regret, watch it pass him by? He was no longer possessed of a morbid curiosity about what stuff through which the leading edge plowed.

Lloyd put the book back in its place. He did not disdain the times. He was a guy who wrote pictures; he was of another age. He had so little in the game that he couldn't feel anything more than benign amusement. Lloyd scratched near where he supposed his "yi'cha," such as it was, might reside and caught himself laughing.

THIRTY-FIVE

HERIN DESHPANDE WAS tearing through the proposal as though he had never seen it before, flipping noisily through pages, snapping them as they turned, breathing hard through his nose as if to make a show of working on it, like he was cramming. He hadn't bothered to get out of his seat when Wally entered his office, merely waved Wally in and pointed to a chair. Pointed. Fuck him.

"What about Gerald?" Wally asked.

"What about him?" Deshpande looked up.

"I assumed I'd be meeting with Gerald Hayden."

"I'm the president of Hayden Offshore, Wally."

"*Hayden* Offshore. You can see how I might get the idea."

"Normally I wouldn't look at proposals like this ... at this stage, Hubert would look at them. Maybe later, regards budgets ... but Gerald asked that I see to it myself as a courtesy to you." Herin turned his attention back to the documents.

Where did these guys buy their clothes, wondered Wally.

They always seemed to be in a crisp new shirt. Was that it? Did they actually put on a brand new shirt every morning? Herin's looked especially fresh and white against his brown skin. And his necktie, the knot was, like, perfectly shaped, the silk shiny as motor oil. Wally's suits never seemed to fit. He didn't know how one picked a tie to match. He didn't even remember what it was your tie was supposed to match.

"Okay," Wally said.

"Who did these drawings? They are fantastic." Herin held up a page for Wally to see. It featured an illustration, the O'Neill Evacuation System Module having seconds earlier slipped its stays, sliding down a terminal rail from the deck of an oil rig, about to plunge into a frigid, frothing sea.

"Des's daughter, Rhonda."

"Des runs the motels, right?"

"Blackmarsh Inn, yeah. Sold the one in Clarenville."

"Why did I think that was Brendan?"

"Brendan was our father."

"Right you are. You can tell Des his daughter has got real talent. They're like...what's the word...*steampunk*."

"Steampunk? I don't think so, she's a good kid, Rhonda."

"No, steampunk is a...type of drawing? No. Or it's a style of..." Herin searched for the word. "Style of style, I guess." He looked back at the drawing. "And the water is definitely referencing *The Great Wave*, that Japanese print, the famous one. Hokusai, right? *The Great Wave*?"

Wally shook his head. What was this Paki getting on about? Deshpande closed up the proposal and handed it across his desk to Wally.

"Fascinating, Wally, but . . . is there a need for a new system?"

"We got better navigation."

"That may well be, but the existing systems are made to standards."

"These are better than those standards."

"You see, Wally, things are only ever made to existing standards. That's sort of the bar at which everyone competes in pricing."

"But we're a local company." Wally did not appreciate Deshpande talking down to him, like Wally didn't know how things worked.

"There are preferences, for sure, but it's an international business. The players are bigger than the countries in which they operate."

"Yeah, but—"

"You might be coming late to the table with this, Wally."

"Yeah . . . but . . . no . . . see . . ."

"You know where there are terrific opportunities?"

"Where?"

"Labrador."

"Labrador?"

"Clear land. We cannot get land cleared on time. And scaffolding. Industrial scaffolding. Crying need for it. Tremendous business opportunity."

"Three days," Wally said, holding up the proposal, now rolled into a club. "These can operate on full power. Seventy-two hours. In heavy seas."

"I don't know much about the engineering side, Wally. Like I said, financing." Herin looked at his watch. "You going to the

Board of Trade luncheon?"

"No."

"Scaffolding, Wally, that's where you want to concentrate. And Labrador."

"Yeah, sure."

"I'm introducing the speaker. I gotta go."

THIRTY-SIX

NOT FOR THE first time, the Board of Trade seated Matt next to its guest speaker. It was part of the job of being mayor. A signed copy of Imogen Hume's *The Music* was on the table in front of him. Her seat was empty now, for she was on stage, giving her address in a serrated Scottish accent.

"Goverrrnment-funded public health care is self-defeating; it extends the lifespan of those most taxing the system. It is fundamentally at odds with nature..."

The "music" of Hume's title was that which we must all face, her book another right-wing *cri de guerre* against the failings of the state, against the fiction of "society." Matt, having forgotten the bumph for this lunch, was looking forward to something more tuneful. How foolish of him.

He thought of his mom, dreamy and beaming, an inch of ash on her Matinee as she bathed in her daily Bach or Rach. He'd walk into the living room and she would smile at him. She was otherwise motionless, all the dancing going on in her eyes.

Unlike Ms. Hume, Matt's mother was pear-shaped. She could and would not wear the shimmering sleeve into which Ms. Hume was snaked. Mom was mousy with hazel eyes and auburn hair. Ms. Hume was lithe, blue-eyed, and Viking raider blond.

Matt opened her book near its middle and read: "...the equivalent moral hazard of bailing out large financial institutions. Pensions are a transparent Ponzi scheme, vital only so long as contributions outstrip withdrawals, that their entirely predictable failure should be underwritten by government only reinforces..."

Applause. Ms. Hume had concluded. Herin Deshpande rose, walked to the podium, and shook her hand. He gave her a tidily wrapped gift box, a modest token of appreciation. Some Newfoundland knickknack, no doubt, something cute and useless anchored by a small beach rock. She made her way to the table. Matt stood to greet her.

MS. HUME ATE every morsel of her lunch. Matt left much of the chalky salmon and sodden veg on his plate. Hume had the sinew of someone who never missed the gym or yoga practice. Hence, thought Matt, the careless appetite.

"When did you come to Canada, Ms. Hume?"

"Grraduate school. Univerrsity of Toronto."

"You studied...?"

"Economics. Maths and models end of it. Grrandiose equations. Gaussian copula function, Black-Scholes equation, things few understand and fewer still find interesting."

Matt knew vaguely of the Black-Scholes equation, a

mathematical formula used to determine risks by determining the range of prices of stock options, or something like that. Matt wondered if it might not be dressed-up conjuring—spells, monetary hexes and charms—but didn't grasp it all well enough to have confidence to say so.

"Me too. Not U of T. Concordia. Not grad school," Matt said.

"You've a degree in economics?"

"Yes."

"Concorrdia? Montrreal?"

"Correct. Scots built the town."

"That so?"

"It is."

"They told me you were a hockey player."

"I was."

"You look like an athlete." Hume smiled at Matt. "That's a compliment."

Matt had not listened to Ms. Hume's speech closely enough and was running out of things to say.

"Do I gather, then, after graduate school...banking?"

She laughed and placed her hand high on Matt's thigh.

"No. I actually ended up working as a comments moderator at the *National Post*, the newspaperr," she said, tightening her grip.

"Comments moderator?"

"You know, when people leave comments on the online version of the stories. They have to be screened. Currrated, essentially." She let go his leg.

"Hate speech and all that."

"Therre was no quarrrel with hate speech; I think that might have accounted for the lion's share of the content. Racist scrreeds, particularly directed against Muslims, were common but not allowed, the obviously libellous ... but hate — ad hominem attack, character assassination — werre all good. The id in idiot." She took a long draught of water. "And it was content the publisher didn't have to pay for. There is a ravenous hunger for content and no one to pay for it. Ravenous."

"Can't have been pleasant."

"It was instructive. Every success I've had since I owe to what I learned about the country on that job. Canadians better betrray themselves in anonymity."

"Like us all."

Ms. Hume leaned forward over her polished-off plate, her head turned so that Matt could not but meet her eye.

"My flight isn't until morrning."

"Connections are difficult here."

"I thought you Newfoundlanderrs had a rreputation for being frriendly."

"I ..."

"Not a grreat to-do, but I'd love a glass of wine and can't drink alone without thinking I've a problem. Scottish."

"I'm married."

"Or course you are. Oh look, Mr. Deshpande beckons. I've people to meet, books to sign. It was a pleasurre, however brief, meeting you." She pushed back her chair and stood.

"The pleasure was mine, Ms. Hume."

"Always read the comments, Mayor Olford," Ms. Hume said and strode away.

THIRTY-SEVEN

THE LARGE, DUTIFULLY cleaned window on to the street put daylight behind the man; his face was the dark side of a moon. His nagging gave him away. Lloyd remembered it from local radio news coverage of City Hall. Councillor Somebody O'Neill was here, on a day boil at the bar at Fiddler's, well into the turn from maudlin to combative. The barmaid had already enlisted, with a glance, a brace of burly regulars to her guard. Somebody O'Neill's newfound friends, beginning to think better of it, were inching out of the widening circle in which they might be splattered or round-housed. O'Neill had cocked his head in Lloyd's direction a few times over the last half hour, but it was his general fouling of the beer parlour's atmosphere that convinced Lloyd to finish this one and vamoose.

"Look at buddy, luh, mainlander."

Lloyd looked back at Councillor Somebody O'Neill but still couldn't see his eyes for the hoary backlight. To answer would be to start a dead-end discussion, in arse pidgin, with this yomyock.

"Are you a mainlander?" O'Neill persisted.

There was nothing to be done for it. Lloyd was about to speak up when his phone chimed a text. It was from Natalie.

"I bought a steak to cook you, Love Nat."

"You looks like a mainlander."

A steak. Lloyd actually told Natalie he was going to the library to do research today. The library!

"Go back to Toronto out of it!"

Lloyd pocketed the phone. He stepped toward O'Neill and saw there wasn't much to the fella. For a moment, after reading Natalie's text, Lloyd fooled himself into thinking he'd happily take a punch, that he deserved one.

"I'm a Notre Dame bayman. So go fuck yourself," said Lloyd, letting the *f* of *fuck* propel a thread of spittle O'Neill's way.

Lloyd turned to the barmaid, said, "Thank you, Geraldine," and left the pub without further incident.

THIRTY-EIGHT

ALESSANDRA SEARCHED FOR, but could not locate, Jule's book. She watched him progress from disorientation to panic to rage.

"Where did you hide it? What's wrong with you? *Connivente puttana!*"

She eventually discovered the missing volume in the crisper drawer of the refrigerator. Romaine lettuce, Goldoni, mottled radishes, heel of Parmesan.

Having the cold book cover in his tremulous hands immediately calmed Jules.

He heeded Alessandra's suggestion that he go to bed. He asked if she was coming too.

"I will in a moment," she said, thinking she did not want to. "Let me lock up."

Later, under the blankets, he put his arms around her and fell into an untroubled sleep.

There was something in the nature of his holding her that was new. It was not conjugal but filial.

THIRTY-NINE

CLUTCHING A FILE relating to the proposed park at Kavanagh Court as a pretext, Matt went looking for Alessandra. He hoped to find her in her office so he might close the door and speak in private. But, Maria, the secretary Alessandra shared with three other councillors, told Matt he had just missed her.

Matt searched the building. By the hour, by the minute, he was losing a clear sense of what had happened between Alessandra and him in the park. There was a spontaneous embrace and a deep, thrilling, kiss. They'd been interrupted by two derelicts walking their dogs. The men were lost in conversation and scarcely glanced at Matt and Alessandra. Matt was sure they had not recognized him, or, if they had, did not care. The moment was so fleeting that it was difficult to recall with any clarity.

Thrilling? Yes, the kiss was thrilling.

Matt was going to apologize to Alessandra, say he was inexplicably overcome and undisciplined and they should...

should what? Matt was then going to put it behind them with a return to business, was going to explain that however objectionable to Alessandra was the selling of naming rights to public spaces it was the new normal, that certain interests had convinced the public that taxation was an evil and so the spending side of the equation was therefore ... well ... that was it, wasn't it? They would agree to disagree on Jerjuice Park, on much else. That should be the nature of their relationship henceforward, cordial but apart.

To stand for election on a platform of greater taxation would take kamikaze courage. To say things plainly, to tell it like it was, was a position no serious candidate could entertain. If he ran for the Conservatives next federal election, Matt would adhere to a script, would preach that taxation was indeed a wrong, would extol family values, free trade, vigilance against terror, would stand for the energy warehouse, hockey and Tim's. If he told Alessandra that he was going to stand for the Conservatives that would surely convince her that kissing him was a terrible mistake, that she was confused by the situation with her husband, that it was an accident, an accident, nobody's fault.

Matt saw Planning Durnford's back through a glass wall and turned on his heels.

Hockey. The Conservatives were going to run him on hockey, of course. Taxation, trade weren't ever going to come into it. They recruited Matt because they didn't think he was that smart. Maybe they got that right.

He decided to take an hour or two and drive out to the Mercedes dealership.

He started the car. The passenger side door opened. Alessandra climbed in.

"Just drive," she said.

NOT KNOWING WHERE else he should go, Matt bore westward in the direction of the car dealerships.

"I am happily married," he said.

"So am I," said Alessandra. "More or less. But that's nothing to do with it."

"No?"

"No. It's something else."

FORTY

IT *WAS* SOMETHING else, it was as shocking as it was natural, it was radiation from the stars, it was hailstones on a blazing hot day. It was as dizzying as whiskey. It stood by itself, untempered by her other feelings for Matt. It was pure and fierce. She knew a want that existed free of anything else, that was its own reason.

"Take us somewhere," she said.

"I think what happened in the park," said Matt, "...it was an accident."

"Not a mistake though."

"No. I don't know."

"Take us somewhere," she said.

"Where!" he shouted, not at Alessandra but through the windshield at the world beyond. "Where in this *village* can I possibly take us?"

FORTY-ONE

IT WAS THORNS. It was a heart attack. His head was pounding. His cock was filling with blood and his balls were tugging a cramp that would twist and tear him in two.

There was a Ramada Inn not five minutes away but it was always the site of some meeting or conference and so familiar faces. There was the Capital but the manager there, Leon Sexton, was on the Board of Trade. The Chateau Park in Mount Pearl? No, the parking lot was right on the street. He turned the car from one street to another, directionless. They were now in a shabby subdivision, amidst bungalows, in a channel walled by vinyl siding.

"Take us somewhere, Matt," she said again.

There was an expansive graveyard out his window. From this elevation he could see east across the city, could see the harbour narrows and the sea beyond. He should turn left and head back to City Hall. He put on the blinker, left.

"I don't think—" he started.

"Then don't," she answered. "I don't need to hear anything about before, or what comes next, okay? Take us somewhere."

He turned right, the car behind blaring its horn at his false indication. He was on Blackmarsh Road and ahead saw the Blackmarsh Inn.

ALESSANDRA HUNG BACK by the entrance to the compact lobby. The place was plain but reasonably clean and well-maintained. The desk clerk was a bulky, grave man in a boxy grey suit Matt could not imagine anyone choosing off the rack. The melancholic motelier, "Des" said his name tag, knew what was going on, of course he did, discretion was his business, and he took pains not to too often look up. He showed no sign of recognizing Matt's face or name and was swift but unhurried with the paperwork.

"Room 107," he said, handing Matt an actual key—not a magnetically stripped card—a heavy metal key dangling from a diamond-shaped hard plastic tab.

ALESSANDRA UNDID HIS belt as they crossed the threshold. She pulled his jacket back off his shoulders with her forehead pressed hard into his chest, as if to gain leverage, putting everything she had into this.

He could not get her out of the dress quick enough so she'd pushed him away, going for a zipper or hasp on the back as if she was reaching for an arrow in a quiver.

He had not enough time to look at her, even though she paused, standing, for a moment after peeling the hose from her legs.

She took hold of his arms at his triceps, above his elbow and she walked backwards, steered him, showing him a dance step, back onto the bed.

And as he'd dreamed, just as he'd dreamed, her knees were up and her hand was on the back of his neck and they were together.

THE MOTEL ROOM viewed from the bed was squat and sordid. There was a static electric felt of dust on the screen of the television. The wallpaper was pimpled, covered with keloids. Matt could hear a winded vacuum in the hallway and steady traffic on the four lanes outside.

So much of the day was pointless repetitions, stacking things up and then knocking them down so you could pick them up again, driving back and forth over the same roads.

His clothes were on the floor; they'd be creased and dirty. He reeked of sex, of spit and cum, and would have to shower. What had he done? He was devoted to his wife, to Patty; they were a family.

Was he mad, had he gone mad?

FORTY-TWO

IIIS WAS THE weight of a wave, like walking into the surf. Bones, locked, had come undone. There'd been a burr of noise in her ears, a roar.

ALESSANDRA NOTICED LIGHT coming from behind the curtains, brilliant filaments fraying in dusty air. The day seemed full, the purpose to merely be in it. There was a warm trickle, sticky as jam, running down her thigh and a burn on her face from his.

Their clothes were decorating the floor of the room like flags, semaphore, surrender, and prayer. Her mouth was sandy. She craved wine and a cigarette. A lover. Take a lover. Matt was devoted to his wife, Alessandra could not remember the woman's name, and he would go back, safely, to his family, and Alessandra needn't think of him until she wanted him again, needed him again.

It was mad, life was mad.

FORTY-THREE

WHERE WAS ALES? She was supposed to be home? Was there an appointment? The doctor was/they kept changing it/ Alessandra's father was a trial/the mother was another story/ her name was...

No/there was something to do with a deer/she said there were deer in the park/venison wine Venice.

Stag? Jules knew to write it down/in the kitchen/on the fridge there was the pad he wrote things on to remember them.

Not to put on the kettle/set an alarm.

Stage, he wrote.

Where was I?

A deer. A ruminant. A horn.

Ruminate.

Deer man was only looking for a place to think/somewhere quiet to sort one's thoughts/the calm of the country for the city was chaos and they kept changing everything.

Ruminate. Chew the cud.

Rumen. Ruminis. Gullet. Guts.

It takes guts.

Guts for garters!

I don't know the whole story.

FORTY-FOUR

THE DAY BEFORE, coming home from Fiddler's, Lloyd opened a
squelchy voice mail from his brother announcing his pending
return from France, less than nine weeks since his departure.
Lloyd was sure Dave had told him he was going for eighty-five
days.

It was Lloyd's intention to hire a housecleaner before his
brother's arrival, but he thought he was near the limit of his
renegotiated bank overdraft. Attempting and failing to with-
draw $200 from an ATM, he learned he was broke. Lloyd was
skint with nowhere to turn.

Everything he needed to tackle the job himself was beneath
the kitchen sink: cleansers as luminous as radium, a bucket,
rubber gloves, brushes, and sponges.

On his knees in the bathroom, scrubbing around the toi-
let, haloed with ammonia, with chlorine and piss, he wondered if this wasn't his future. Poor Harry Davenant became
a security guard. Lloyd naively held teaching as his last resort,

believing that positions were easy to come by. Dupes were forever going to seminars and classes to learn how to write screenplays. People who would never imagine writing a novel after reading one, or a play after seeing one, could still easily convince themselves they knew how to make a movie having dozed through a few. Only too late did Lloyd learn that experience in the film and television business counted for naught in the Academy. They were more likely to give a job to someone who garnered a Ph.D. studying *cinema* than making pictures. Some regional colleges stooped to having English profs lecture on the craft.

And to conduct one of those high-priced screenwriting seminars one first had to concoct some hare-brained theory concerning the structure of filmed stories. They were parabolic or played in seven and a half acts or the characters were spirit vectors or the mouse takes the fucking cheese.

Gripping the fat lip of the porcelain bowl, Lloyd pushed himself up off the tiled floor.

He stood over his guest bed wondering if he should strip it now or tomorrow. Whether he was going to spend one more night here at his Hôtel d'Alsace or take up Natalie's offer of dinner, an invitation he assumed included a sleep over. He didn't yet know. He would check his emails and then revisit the question.

The Facebook page he'd created had taken on a life of its own. Lloyd no longer needed to feed it, to bait and prompt. A dynamic online community, The Deer Friends, had grown around the cause of Harry Davenant. They all stood by Harry's choice and took this shared belief as an opportunity to post pictures of themselves and share other items distantly related to the matter of the one-time thespian's adventure of self-discovery in the park. Lloyd had an aversion to having his picture taken and considered sharing images of oneself on the Internet unimaginably vulgar; taking one's own picture and then sharing it with the world was pathological. There were actors for that. It was another attitude that seemed to put him further and further outside social norms.

There was chatter among the Deer Friends of creating a fawn-coloured ribbon and an adhesive ribbon-like sticker for the back of one's car that would show support for Harry. But the Friends were such an amorphous group, so *virtual*, that no one took the initiative to have anything made. The fawn ribbon would be worn, like a bandage, in the mind.

There were, Lloyd learned from the Facebook page, folks all over in various states of transitioning from man to beast. There were two people in Ontario, one in Thunder Bay, another in Orillia, whose advocates took pains to clarify were not suffering hypertrichosis—that is, did not have "werewolf syndrome" but were, at heart, wolves. There was a man in Sydney Mines, Nova Scotia, who wanted it made equally clear that he was a werewolf and not a wolf. Several nuns of the same order at a Karmelitenkloster in Graz, Austria, were accepting that they were goats. A woman in Vancouver and another in Calgary were "cat people" in the truest sense. There was only one other deer out there, a woman in California, whose husband seemed, genuinely, to be looking for someone of the same species to keep her company. A group of deer, Lloyd discovered, was called a *mob*.

Today there was a flurry of complaints on the Facebook page concerning an anonymous mock Twitter feed, one purporting to be the social media voice of Harry himself. It called itself Feral Theatric. Lloyd dared to see for himself:

After cull enrages 'Save Bambi' crowd, B.C. creates $100k/year 'advisory committee' on urban deer http://natpo.st/1LYcgWH

Disney's deer was a frequent theme. Another tweet came with a link to a clip from the movie, Thumper saying, If you can't say something nice don't say nothing at all.

Another coupled to YouTube and some Elizabethan minstrel group calling itself The Bare Naked Ladies singing "The Deer Song" from a Stratford Theatre production of *As You Like It*:

> *What shall he have that killed the deer?*
> *His leather skin and horns to wear.*
> *Then sing him home.*
> *(The rest shall bear this burden.)*
> *Take thou no scorn to wear the horn.*
> *It was a crest ere thou wast born.*
> *Thy father's father wore it,*
> *And thy father bore it.*
> *The horn, the horn, the lusty horn*
> *Is not a thing to laugh to scorn.*

Another led clickers to a news story about a Saskatoon couple's fight to keep a raccoon as a pet, with Fake Harry's comment: "Being petted is so degrading. And there are things

I could tell you about raccoons..."

Lloyd thought tweets were supposed to be concise but these, together, constituted a staccato aggregation of spurious connections. The big screen had surrendered to the small screen, which was giving way to the smallest screens, those held in hand or dancing on laps. They were hysteria accelerators as much as they were communications devices. The medium wasn't the message, it was the mania. Lloyd closed the Twitter box but it only got worse.

Next on the Facebook page was a threat. Below a logo, the stylized mountain lion — ears back, lips curled, fangs forward — of an outfit calling itself Animal Separation was the message: YOU ARE HOMOSAPIEN ASSIMILATORS. ANIMALS ARE SOVEREIGN. ANIMALS DO NOT SERVE. ANIMALS ARE APART. STAY OUT OF THE FOREST.

What idiots, thought Lloyd. Did they imagine that Harry had defected to the deer side and people were trying to lure him back to humanity? Or make Harry into a double agent for the opposable thumbers? Or that...what? Jaysus, it was that sort of unknowable dumb, that kind of obtuseness that came in an iron dome. Lloyd had been altogether too clever. His prank, he sensed, was coming back to bite him, literally perhaps, in the ass. If people learned they were nursing a delusion of Lloyd's invention they would surely lynch him.

And while Lloyd's phone number may have been deleted from the speed dials of Hollywood, had been wilfully forgotten in his trade, he had not been bestowed with the gift of invisibility. Lloyd's was the indignity of having vanished *with* a trace. The nutters could easily track him.

People delighted in their outrage, thought Lloyd, a notion that compelled him to smoke. He went out onto the rotting wooden stairs from the backyard to the rear door and lit up.

Professional storytelling worked best when it was the earliest transcription of the zeitgeist. You couldn't tell the people out there in television land a better new story than their own. Lloyd's little improv about Harry . . . well, *his lie* about Harry . . . got such traction because people out there could see themselves running from their homes, their jobs, and their family and into the woods.

There was a show in it, no? Perhaps not of the kind Lloyd fancied, but times changed and one had to adapt. Factual Entertainment. Unscripted Drama. It was the kind of thing Mike Vargas liked to hear pitched these days. If Harry was up-to-date with his Actors Guild dues then maybe . . .

Lloyd took his phone from his shirt pocket and lifted his specs up to his bald pate so he could read the tiny print on the touchscreen. Letter by letter, his digit too fat for accurate strokes, he answered Natalie's invitation. "A stesk *steak* soumds *sounds* grest *great*. What rime *time?*"

FORTY-FIVE

SHOULD HAVE BEEN laying smacks to that mainlander's face. Wally would have too, if buddy hadn't walked out of the bar. And then the barmaid giving Wally the gears. Shit on Fiddler's. Was the place even up to code? Wally was going to see there was an inspection. And woe betide 'em they applied for some permit from the city. Wally had lots of loyal friends in the Engineering Department. Buddy said he was from Notre Dame Bay. Yeah, right. Dressed like a quiff, white jacket and pants. Was he going on safari? Quiff. Should've put a glass right in his ear. No hesitation and swinging for the one on the other side of his head. Like Brendan told him, never mind your hands, deal with that later, let that rum tumbler explode in his ear and then whale on buddy, don't stop until you're so baffed-out you can't throw another punch or land another kick.

Wally was in his truck and already to the Ruby Line so thought, shag it all, go get the quad, put 'er aboard, and take 'er for a spin down to the Skin Tilt. Get away from cock-eating

St. John's. He needed it.

And Herin Deshpande, Wally was going to have to watch that Paki, make sure the O'Neill Evacuation System didn't show up in a few years as Herin's idea. And what about Gerry Hayden, ditching him, leaving Deshpande to tell Wally to go to Labrador out of it? Brother Des wanted to hear, "right away," what Gerald Hayden's answer was, but Wally didn't have the heart to phone him after the meeting. Des had been calling Wally all day but Wally hadn't answered.

Quad was in the shed at Des's place. If Des was home from the motel Wally would deliver the bad news in person, when he was getting the machine.

FORTY-SIX

NEWFOUNDLAND WAS BEAUTIFUL, stunning, get no argument
on that score from Gary. Flying in the first time, the Airbus
banked over the sea and turned back for the airport so Gary
could see the unassailable cliffs plunging into the cold cold
waters. There were hues of blue and green and grey down
there *with weight*, colours Gary did not know existed. But the
Newfies were hell-bent on despoiling their outpost. Gary had
never seen so much litter. He'd never seen so much garish
roadside signage — firewood, road salt, discount nail salons.
He never got over how ugly were the buildings in St. John's.
There were a few lovely decorated cakes clinging to the hills
in the downtown, but the drive down the Ruby Line to his
house in the Southlands took him past one heap of shit after
another. The area to the west of the city was once agricul-
tural, hay fields and rows of cabbage and potato running to
treed hills, *goulds*, nearer the coastline. You'd think the setting would inspire them to erect something attractive, but no,

they flung up metal sheds and baby barns and the worst sort of suburban tract housing. They shared a love of the two-car garage — most of the houses seemed built around them, great thrusts of garage out to meet the street. They worshipped the road, never setting houses back on their lots, but coming as close to the pavement as possible. This, Gary now knew, after a few months policing the place, was not for economic reasons but so they could better reconnoitre one another's comings and goings. They were so goddamned prying and meddlesome. He couldn't get to Arizona soon enough.

The police radio announced there was a vehicular pursuit in progress, four cars chasing a female suspect in a Ford Focus. More action Gary wasn't seeing.

Gary would torture himself by counting the number of pickup trucks on the road carrying nothing in the back. Newfies wanted a truck even if they had no call for one. Gary supposed it was to do with the oil economy, people needing to believe they were part of it by donning the costume. Today, on the way home, Gary was one-for-twenty-one. He'd counted twenty-one pickups and only one, carrying a large, grey plastic fish box, being used for the purpose for which it was designed.

The pickup ahead of him now made it a record, one-for-twenty-two and, as a bonus, it was weaving in and out of its lane, the driver either looking at a phone or impaired. Gary didn't need this but there wasn't much waiting for him home in the Southlands; he was on call so couldn't even look forward to a beer. He activated the light on the dash and gave the siren a couple of cycles. The driver took a moment to realize Gary was there, probably listening to music. The truck straightened up, the driver put on his blinker telling Gary that he was looking for a place to pull over. The truck slowed and turned down a dirt lane of an abandoned farm.

The track was so narrow that the pickup had to continue over the rutted way past the boarded-up homestead to find a spot to park. Tree branches, maple and some apple, scraped the side of Gary's car, making a sound he found oddly reassuring, recalling trips to the countryside of Ontario with his family when he was a boy. There was a clearing ahead, enough space to turn farm machinery around, and the remnants of an old barn, its roof collapsed. The truck stopped there. It seemed a sensible place, out of traffic, suggesting to Gary that the driver wasn't drunk but distracted. Gary knew he should call in and run the plate number but that would mean paperwork later. He would see if there was any sign of intoxication and if not simply give the guy a warning. That way he'd be home sooner.

FORTY-SEVEN

THIS WAS THE end; an impaired charge would ruin Wally. It would be all over the news. Trina was looking for a reason to leave him, he knew it, and she'd been ragging him about the drink. He'd refuse the breathalyzer. No, that was as bad. Pretend he was stricken? Having a heart attack or taking some sort of fit.

He knew this place — the Lucys owned the land and rented it to hay farmers. When old Tom Lucy died, his youngsters wanted nothing to do with it, didn't want cow shit on their shoes, couldn't even be bothered to lease it and they let it go to seed. Now the land was worth a fortune. Wally'd seen the plans for the subdivision that was going up here, the water and sewer was going to cost the city a mint because of the elevation. Tom Lucy's children and grandchildren did nothing for it; they owned it because it was given to them. And what did Wally get? Nudding! What did the O'Neills have? Fuck-all in a brin bag.

If he slowed this thing with the cop down, called his lawyer, stalled for a hour, would he clear .08? How many did he have in him? Couple of beers and then rum and Coke. Three drinks? One...two...No! He'd had five rum and Cokes.

Run for it? Wally's truck could probably get across the fields but the ghost car would hold up in the mud. Cop would call in others on patrol; they'd nab him on the other side. Would they? How long would they take to get here?

In the side mirror he saw the cop getting out of his car.

FORTY-EIGHT

THE AIR WAS humid and smelled of manure. Nearby crows were in dispute.

Arizona was the desert. Was landlocked. Was hotter than this but bone dry. Gary was ready for such a change, a big one, a new life, really. Despite the cost, the disruption of the move from Toronto he'd been obliged to make, despite his want of children, of a family, getting another life was not an opportunity given many people.

Blue 2012 Dodge Ram, plate number HBX 237.

Would Gary be a changed man in Embustero? Would he present himself differently? He would treat himself to new clothes, a whole new wardrobe. "Clothes really do make the man," Eugene had told Gary when they were working up his legend for the G20 operation.

The night after Eugene arrived in St. John's to tell Gary they would accommodate his request to relocate, Gary had gone online to look at a couple of singles dating services in the Tucson area.

First drops of rain. He...

The truck lunged. Gary heard the engine and the tires tearing up the dirt, stones spraying the undercarriage. It was in reverse, coming for him. Before he could move the corner of the bed was in him.

Tonnage of corner, like a house turned inside out.

His chest was gone. He felt that. He was on his back. His left arm was not right.

This was serious.

He was in trouble.

To breathe was.

Blood blood.

Dodge Ram. Room 22.

Plate number 126 246 163.

One of the crows.

Catch my breath.

Policeman.

Someone please call my brother 905 237 911 please call.

The sea was so cold in Newfoundland you couldn't swim in it.

Everything was going to be fine. All good.

This is.

Another cr

FORTY-NINE

FROM HER BED or her desk at work Patty more and more frequently heard the cry of emergency vehicles' sirens. They weren't nearly so common in years past, she thought.

Today there'd been a terrific commotion outside the office, a knot of trouble that closed down the intersection nearest the parking lot in front of the Atlantech offices.

A police chase had ended with a collision. Patty and a few others went outside in time to witness the arrest. A woman, in her thirties, Patty guessed, was hauled from a small Ford, a gash on her head flooding mounded blond dreadlocks, turning them henna brown. There were tattoos on her neck. She was shoeless, in track pants with a brand emblazoned across the seat. Put roughly up against her car she was handcuffed with quick skill and then swarmed by hands in blue latex. Fight had first lifted the woman but as it departed she grew heavy as stone. The police dragged her to the caged back seat of a cruiser.

What were this woman's crimes, Patty wondered, and how would she atone for them?

Jesus forgave but God judged. Only now did Patty see that God's mercy was his judgement. That all was measured, tallied, and accounts settled did more than reward the righteous. It was the only means by which justice and free will could reside in the same house.

Judgement was the pure and final weighing of things.

We did not understand it. Pastor Maggs himself was vain to assert that he did. It wasn't religion at all; it was scientific. Nature punished the wicked.

Moral codes were not invented or imagined, they were not prescribed. They were observed in every sense of that word. Observance. You know what is right. You know what is true. Relativism meant chaos. What was evil? Chaos. Chaos was evil. The devil was disorder. A bloom was order. The tides were order. Turmoil came from the unravelling. To be judged was an entreaty to be in order. Prayer was a plan of action, a schedule. Prayer was a to-do list.

Was it kind to forgive the sinner? No, it was actually kinder that they be castigated. To leave ill deeds unpunished was to leave the burden on those who committed them.

Punishment was salt on meat.

Was there any greater passion than wrath?

FIFTY

ALESSANDRA WASN'T BEING particularly discreet. She took the time to stop in the middle of the Blackmarsh Inn parking lot to search through her handbag, concerned, Matt supposed, that she'd left something behind in the motel room.

Matt noticed a car from Sentry, the security company, and wondered if they'd taken down the number of his licence plate and realized, quickly, that such a notion was absurd.

AT EVERY RED light during the drive back downtown, Matt worried someone stopped in the next lane was going to look into the car and see him, the mayor, with Alessandra and put it together that they'd minutes before been in bed at a motel in the west end.

They were on Topsail Road heading east toward City Hall when she asked, "Why were you looking for me?"

"I don't..."

"Maria said you were looking for me. I came back to my

office, you'd been there...presumably not to propose we go have a fuck at the Blackmarsh Inn?"

Jaysus, she was laughing, this was all a grand lark for her. She'd rolled the window down to let the summer air get in her hair. She'd donned her big round sunglasses and was smiling at the heat of the sun on her face.

"No. I was going to talk about the naming rights issue, Kavanagh Court," Matt said.

"So ridiculous."

"I think it's...it's the way it's done these days."

"Then we leave it undeveloped, a grove of trees," she said. "That might even be better. It would. 'Parks' — that's someone telling you how to enjoy nature. Bad as a zoo, if you think about it. Leave it."

"I don't think Council will even understand what you are saying."

"Forget them, Matt. They are such clowns. Is there any way we can go for a glass of wine?"

"A glass of wine? Now? I don't think so. We have to be careful. Are you going back to City Hall?"

"No. If we can't get a drink I should go home. Play nursemaid."

"I don't know where you live."

"Oh." Alessandra sounded surprised, as though now knowing one another as they did could not jibe with knowing so little about one another. "Rennie's Mill Road."

As they neared Alessandra's house Matt asked, "Where should I let you out?"

"In front." Alessandra was puzzled by Matt's question.

"Okay, sure."

He pulled up to the curb and put the car in park. Alessandra opened the door and then turned back and, taking his head in her hands, kissed him on the mouth.

"Nobody saw anything," she said, and laughed again as she climbed out on to the sidewalk.

FIFTY-ONE

COMING IN THE front door of his house Matt heard no sounds of life. He made straight for the shower.

At the top of the stairs he heard Patty's voice coming from behind the closed door of their bedroom. She was speaking with someone. On the phone with one of the kids or her sister?

But why had she closed the door?

Matt caught himself hoping that Patty might be in their marriage bed with another man, that he could catch her cheating and that he would forgive her and they would move on.

He thought he would open the door and make a sign that he wasn't going to interrupt and was going to take a shower.

As his hand reached for the knob he heard that Patty was not talking to Katie or Jack or Fiona. "Today, Lord, I learned again it was..." she said.

Patty would hear the water running, Matt reasoned, and know it was him. There was no reason to intrude on her conversation with the maker.

PATTY WAS SEATED at the dining table fussing with her iPhone.

"You took a shower."

"I felt gross."

"That Deer Man is back in Bowring Park."

"I think he's in the hospital," said Matt.

"No, they let him out. It's on Facebook," said Patty.

"I didn't know."

"It is sick, the whole thing."

"You've said before. I'll grant you it is mighty peculiar but—"

"It's more than peculiar, Matthew, it's deviant, to be taken over by an animal, to be . . ."

"To be *what*, Pats?"

"I thought you were going to do something about it."

"I did what I could," he said. "We contacted the police."

"Well, he's still there."

Patty laid down her iPhone and slid it across the table, pushing it away.

"These phones, it's a form of idolatry," she said.

"I suppose, in a way, yes it is."

"And Apple? It's a cult. It's like a consumption cult."

"A cult, Pats? I think that's taking it a bit far."

"I'm cooking salt fish for supper, with potatoes and scrunchions."

"Not with tomato and olives?"

"Do you prefer it that way?"

"No. I like both. I love fish and potatoes."

"Never had it any other way growing up than with fatback and onions and drawn butter," Patty said as she stood and went to the kitchen.

FIFTY-TWO

GOING THROUGH THE change, Trina was hot as a woodstove, and with a fever of dread running through him and his guts a-boil Wally was burning up in his bed. He went downstairs and lay on the couch.

His trial would be brief and sordid. Upon conviction and the harsh sentencing that was dealt those who killed a policeman, he would be shipped to a horrific prison on the mainland. Were there Newf networks within those tall walls? No, they were too small in numbers; the demographic crisis, the decline of the Newfoundlanders would be as clear to see behind bars as it was around the bay. And having run over one of their law and order cousins, the guards would not protect Wally. Wally would be the plaything of sadistic natives. They would revenge the extinction of the Beothuks on his sorry Catholic ass.

Wally began to tremble. He had to put this panic away; he wasn't caught yet. He needed to appear calm to avoid arousing suspicion. What was there to link him to the corpse on Lucy's farm? It might still be lying there, unfound, the trail colder and colder. He needed to put his mind to something that would settle it, so he made himself think on the O'Neill Evacuation System. Like sucking on dumbtit, rolling those pictures in his head always soothed Wally. He saw the rivets and thick windows, the hull a coat of armour. He imagined it dropping from the rig into an ocean churned up into curds and disappearing for a moment beneath the surface and rising, buoying up, and the powerful motor turning the screws to convey it safely to open water. The storm raged but the boat was unsinkable, it rode waves as big as office towers and within, strapped to his seat, snug, safe, unsinkable Wally saw himself so at ease that he could let his eyes close and rest, could feel the vessel on the currents, hear the ocean as you would in a shell to your ear.

FIFTY-THREE

Haldeman Estates
301 Locura Canyon Road
Enredo, California
93446

Meredith Devereaux
Director, Parks and Recreation (acting)
City of St. John's
10 New Gower Street
P.O. Box 908
St. John's, NL
Canada
A1C 5M2

Dear Ms. Devereaux,
I have read with great interest about the man transitioning to deer who lives, unharrassed, in a civic park in your city.

Some years ago my beloved wife, Hildy, and I confronted and ultimately accepted the fact that she too was a deer. We live on a large, award-winning winery near Paso Robles that, until recently, easily accommodated her needs to roam and forage. By 2009 Hildy was living happily here as a hind.

In 2011 we had a brush fire in the area that badly spooked Hildy. The smoke and flames drove her and other wildlife deep into the rough terrain of the Santa Lucia coastal mountain range. I thought I'd lost her. When she finally returned, after an absence of ten days, she was in poor condition and had to receive medical treatment against her will.

One impact of climate change is the certainty that such brush fires are going to be a regular feature of life in this area of California. Further, recent drought has greatly increased the risk of contracting coccidioidomycosis, or Valley Fever, a potentially life-threatening respiratory condition caused by the inhalation of fungus endemic to the area. All mammals are vulnerable. As you probably know, we live on a major fault in the earth. Earthquakes are a significant cause of the soil disruption that allows the spores to be disseminated.

Other than refuelling stops at the Goose Bay Air Base, I have never been to Newfoundland and know of it only what I have read and heard from fellow U.S. Service men. My father was stationed, briefly, at Fort Pepperall during his military service, but I never heard him speak about it.

I judge, given the acceptance shown by your community, that your Bowring Park might provide a more suitable habitat for my wife than California.

As you likely know, deer are not precisely pack or herd animals but are social. I would stay as near as possible to Hildy as she was introduced to the new environment and accept that the buck in your park will assert himself as the dominant male.

Obviously our first visit would be on a trial basis, and if Hildy was happy there I would next have to apply for Canadian residency.

I am wondering if such is possible and what would be the requirements of the City of St. John's for Hildy's relocation.

Sincerely,
Frank Haldeman, BC (ret.)

FIFTY-FOUR

THEY WOULD NOT be like menstrual cramps. Her breasts would get sore—her sisters had bayed complaints when they delivered their brats. Natalie kept checking to see if her nipples were darkening. The time was coming, it was. She would buy one of those home tests at the pharmacy, have it at the ready, and then, once she had the results, make an appointment with Dr. Haroun.

She had tried for years to stop herself thinking of it, of fretting over the prudence of doing it any later in life, of some date beyond which it would be problematic, risky, and then, finally, of having no more eggs.

Every rationalization, every green reason she'd concocted not to was now, suddenly, absurd. Of course one did; it was the most natural thing of all and having only one child was not an affront to the planet. This wasn't the Anthropocene extinction; this honoured something spiritual.

She never had the response to babies that a woman was

supposed to, or at least obliged to. She found them vaguely repellent in being so poorly formed and helpless and mewling. She trusted such could not be the case with her own.

Her sister Martha had been calling over the past few days but Natalie had decided against picking up. There would come a point when one announced it and until then she would not speak with her controlling, judgemental family. Her mind was racing. She would buy a house in St. John's, perhaps in the Georgestown neighbourhood, but one with a larger yard. The child could not be indoctrinated in the public school system. She would start investigating the options. Home schooling was definitely the way to go but Natalie had problems with some of math's orthodoxies. Surely, though, there was an alternative math, a natural math. She would not vaccinate; she could not take that risk. And a name...a name, a Tuskaweegee name, a fierce Tuskaweegee warrior name. Maybe she would have one of those natural "pond births" everyone was talking about...though the water would probably still be very cold in Newfoundland in May.

Owing to circumstances of his career and an unfortunate love life before he met Natalie, fatherhood was a happiness hitherto denied Lloyd. He might be a little old for it but Natalie knew he would be overjoyed when it happened.

FIFTY-FIVE

PATTY THOUGHT HER boss, Joel, suffered from that condition, that high-functioning autism thing. It impaired his ability to communicate. He never made eye contact and could be distracted by something on his computer screen and abruptly ignore you. He sometimes made a noise like a small dog's bark and always laughed at the wrong part of a funny story. And he was too young, however smart he was, to be anyone's boss. He knew not enough of life. Joel pretty much ignored Patty, grunted the occasional instruction as he dumped papers on her desk. One day Patty was just as happy for it, the next put off. Joel did not respect his elders. He did not understand boundaries. Patty had seen him reach, without asking, into someone else's lunch and sample it. He was always curt to the point of rudeness.

"So...here it is," Joel said. Asperger's, that was the name for his condition, Patty remembered. "Stuff, like some routine office stuff, some filing and stuff like paying the rent, is not getting done. And the packaging of that bid for the St . . . Stat . . . Statoil project was a real m-mess, all the numbers in the index were wrong, there was a page missing."

Patty's neck burned. She had forgotten the rent.

"Page 229 was missing. But I talked about this with Paula," Joel continued, "and it's, you know, new for you. It's a new development. So I, and maybe you won't like this, Paula said you would be angry, but I st-started creeping your computer."

"You did what?"

"I monitored how you were spending your time on *our* computer at your d-desk."

"That's an invasion of my privacy, Joel."

"No, I checked with the lawyer, and where it's our computer, company property under the terms of your contract, we are within our rights. And this is finding a solution, okay. Paula said to 'find a solution,' that I am to 'find solutions,' and . . . like, you are not being disciplined, you are not being f-fired. But see, and this is recent, you are spending hours, hours every day on the Internet on un-work-related things, Patty. On this Christian thing y-you are into, on getting recipes, on click bait shit."

"I'm sorry. I guess it's true."

"It happens. Porn, all the time. You have to say, 'I'm not paying you to watch porn.' The young engineers, guys on work terms, always. It's a thing. Internet addiction is a thing."

"I will . . ."

"Something like this happened with my mom. She had a personality change."

"My personality hasn't changed, Joel, I . . ."

"No, no, no . . . this was, with my mother, this was a

menopause thing. Personality, hormones or something, right."

Patty contemplated picking something up off Joel's desk, something hard and sharp, and leaping on him, pummelling him.

"Joel," she said. "Stop there. I am not menopausal."

"Whatever, I'm only saying…"

"Won't happen again."

"Then that is excellent and I will tell Paula that we found a solution."

"I will do all that is expected of me and more. I'm sorry about having been a little distracted these past few months."

"Okay, that's the solution."

STILL BURNING WITH embarrassment, Patty sat at her desk and took stock. Joel was correct. She had fallen far behind, and even as she started in on the backlog of work Patty resisted a desire to go online to check the bulletin board on her church's website, www.cmacan.org, and to look at her Facebook page. She was unable to imagine, without the inspiration of her bookmarked food blogs, what to prepare for supper. Joel was right; it was an addiction.

Patty thought she would get done what had to be done and then reward herself with an hour's surfing, but this, she realized, was the sort of bargain alcoholics made with themselves. She had a problem. She would pray to God for the strength to fight the Internet.

It was after eight before Patty felt she'd caught up enough to leave the office. She had not called Matt to tell him she would be late because she somehow felt that he shared the blame for her bad day. Even as Patty knew this was not the case she held it like a grudge. At ten to seven Matt called her, but she didn't pick up and responded, instead, with a text: "wking late eat without me." Patty didn't want to talk to him. Would she even tell Matt of her humiliation?

She set the security system alarm and locked the front doors of the offices behind her. The dry cleaners next down had closed at six and shed no light. The one-time convenience store next door was still boarded. One of the things she'd neglected to do was to write the landlord and express concern about the deteriorating condition of that part of the property. Like vermin to garbage the failed business was drawing undesirable elements. Unsavoury characters had been spotted lurking around, whether to buy and sell drugs or sex was unknown. If there was no new occupant soon Joel, Paula, and Feodor, the owners of Atlantech, were going to consider moving.

The sun was below the horizon but still tinting the undersides of low clouds. The street lights had come on.

Walking to her Yaris she noticed another car parked on the lot, an Audi. There seemed, at first, no one inside, but as she got closer Patty could make out a form at the wheel. The Audi was in shade, the windows made reflective by the direction and play of the light, so that only when swept by the headlights of a passing car did Patty get a fleeting glimpse inside. There were branches coming from the beast's head, and where would have been eyes there were only punctures in pitch. It looked nowhere, said nothing, and still spoke to Patty at her nerves; it coursed through her and filled her throat till she might choke. She struggled to get in her car, her fingers lacking any grip, her arms weak. She felt as though she might faint, only finding her breath as she drove from the lot onto the street. She heard the blare of car horns as she narrowly missed being struck by oncoming traffic and found, stopped at the next light, her face was wet with tears of dismay and shame.

FIFTY-SIX

CONSTABLE KEVIN MAHER did not see why Chief Cahill thought it should fall to him to clean out Gary Mackenzie's desk. They'd ridden together a few times but it wasn't like they were partners. They certainly weren't friends, despite Kevin's best efforts. Gary was cold, really, didn't seem to much like people. Gathering up Mackenzie's belongings so they could be shipped back to Ontario was a punishment for an infraction he had not committed. It was supposed to be Joanne's job but she was "too upset" apparently, like she knew the guy any better than anyone else at the cop shop.

There was a coffee mug with an image of a Newfoundland dog, its massive tongue lolling. Did he put that in the banker's box? Would it have any meaning to Gary's family up on the mainland? Perhaps it would only remind them of his end. Kevin packed it. He chucked a half bottle of aspirin and a Mars bar. Ring of keys went in the box. There was a glossy brochure for new homes in a gated community — Gran Vista in Embustero,

Arizona. Perhaps it was where Gary meant to retire. Kevin was already counting the years until he could return to his hometown of Pacquet. Policing wasn't what he'd thought it would be. Half of it was social work, in which he had no interest.

There were a number of case files on Gary's desk. Kevin was to sort and list these for Chief Cahill's scrutiny.

Fourth in the stack was the file on the gentleman Gary and Kevin had apprehended in Bowring Park. There was an attached psychiatric assessment. Kevin sat down to read it.

Psychiatric Report
Re: DAVENANT, Harry

Identifying Data
Mr. Davenant is a 61-year-old gentleman who lives on 72 Cochrane Street in St. John's, Newfoundland. Until recently he was employed as a security guard. Patrolling Bowring Park was among his responsibilities. For many years Mr. Davenant was an administrator at the LSPU Theatre in downtown St. John's and before that a professional actor. He is unmarried and has no children.

Chief Complaint
Mr. Davenant was never forthcoming with information during the examination. The greater part of his personal and medical history had to be gleaned from records.

History of Presenting Illness
Mr. Davenant was brought to Waterford Psychiatric

Emergency on July 11, 2013 at 9:15 p.m. after apprehension by police. Mr. Davenant was dwelling in Bowring Park, without shelter, for some weeks and was charged with trespassing. Owing to anecdotal accounts that Mr. Davenant believed he was a deer or other animal and because of his repeated refusals to heed demands that he leave the park after hours the arresting officer judged Mr. Davenant delusional and conveyed him to the psychiatric emergency department.

Though the arresting officer reported Mr. Davenant fled from police he did not resist when finally apprehended, after a lengthy foot chase, in a heavily wooded area near the park's western boundary.

Owing to many weeks living outdoors Mr. Davenant appeared in poor condition. This proved mostly to do with the state of his clothing. Once he was prevailed upon by the assigned nursing aide to shower and provided with clean clothing Mr. Davenant did not have any signs of exposure to the elements or appear to be malnourished. Medical records indicate that he has lost 16 kilograms body weight since his last routine examination three years ago. At that time he was judged to be overweight with marginal blood sugars and cholesterol.

Review of Systems

He denied having hallucinations. He seemed without obsessions or compulsions. Not unlike many men his age he holds some generalized resentment and even anger with regards to the state of contemporary society. He made disparaging remarks about Newfoundland "Newfie Nignogs" and Canada being "a culture on ice."

Mr. Davenant denied ever believing he was a deer. He was perplexed by this line of inquiry and began losing patience with the examining physician when it was pursued.

Current Medications

Mr. Davenant was prescribed Lipitor for high cholesterol but ceased taking it sometime in the last three months, complaining that it made his legs stiff and walking difficult.

Psychiatric History

No evidence of psychiatric disorder. No psychiatric hospitalizations. Mr. Davenant complained of mild depression during a routine medical examination in 2008 but declined medication or psychotherapy. Reported at that time family history of depression on father's side—a beloved uncle, resident in Mr. Davenant's native England, committed suicide in 1983.

Substance Use History

Medical records indicate some infrequent marijuana use. Family physician suggested Mr. Davenant was occasionally drinking to excess. No indication of chronic alcoholism.

Social and Developmental History

Mr. Davenant appears to have had a rich social network that has unravelled somewhat in recent years, leading to a degree of isolation. Mr. Davenant is homosexual and has on two occasions been in stable long-term relationships. A partner died of AIDS-related illness in 1999. Mr. Davenant has never tested positive for HIV. Mr. Davenant's last partner died in an automobile accident in 2009. It appears Mr. Davenant has lived alone since.

Both Mr. Davenant's parents and an older brother are deceased. Mr. Davenant has a younger sister with whom he has had no contact in over 20 years.

With respect to his education, he is a graduate of the Royal Academy of Dramatic Arts in the United Kingdom.

Legal Record

Charge of Disturbing the Peace and Public Mischief stemming from incident at a house party in 1986.

Physical Exam

Mr. Davenant seemed to have some stiffness in the joints (intern mistook as waxy flexibility but this was discounted by the attending psychiatrist) but this diminished over the course of the physical examination. Slight cloudiness in left eye. Old collar-bone break not properly set.

There was some slight bruising on his neck and shoulders.

Recent minor skin abrasions were likely incurred during his pursuit, through heavy brush, by the police.

Mental Status Examination

Overall, Mr. Davenant is a 61-year-old gentleman. As previously noted Mr. Davenant's clothing was ragged and filthy. Otherwise his hygiene was surprisingly good given his recent living conditions. He was withdrawn and unco-operative at the beginning of the interview, refusing to answer questions. When it was pointed out that his failure to answer questions would certainly result in his being admitted he reluctantly provided answers. He was never fully engaged. He was borderline hostile at the beginning of the interview but became somewhat more co-operative. His mood was depressed. His affect appeared withdrawn at the beginning of the interview. No tearfulness. When compelled to speak Mr. Davenant's speech rate and volume were below normal limits. His thought process was clear. There were no loose associations, tangential thinking, or thought blocking. No signs of thought disorder.

Psychiatric Impression

Mr. Davenant is depressed and in need of treatment. Mr. Davenant is in good physical condition for a man of his age and profile. His time living out of doors and changes to his diet have resulted in many improvements to his physical condition. Whether such would continue to be the case cannot be ascertained here. Posing no evident danger to himself or others there is no means of compelling him to seek treatment for his depression or to admit him. Mr. Davenant refused to commit to returning to his home.

The arresting officer's report that Mr. Davenant was delusional and suffering from lycanthropy is without foundation and likely the result of suggestion.

Mr. Davenant reluctantly accepted the assistance of a social worker. As Mr. Davenant has no family in Newfoundland the caseworker took it upon herself to contact some friends who arranged to meet Mr. Davenant upon discharge. He was discharged with no plan for psychiatric follow up. Without therapy and/or medication to treat his depression and underlying anxiety Mr. Davenant does not have a good prognosis.

FIFTY-SEVEN

From: MKJKDean@gattel.ix
To: NatSomm@sympatico.ca
Subject: Trust Issues

Nat,

I feel terrible delivering this message via email but I have to assume you are not answering if your caller ID tells you that it's me calling or something.

Bit of an emergency sitch, so you are going to have to get back to me ASAP. The company has had some serious reversals — catastrophe wouldn't be an exaggeration. The latest is that both Robbar Industrial and Gattel, the holding company, are going to be put in receivership and that the trust may be responsible for losses.

It's become clear that the problem is mostly to do with poor business decisions made by Andrew, keeping the plants in Ontario when we should have outsourced, and poor choices on the retail end (this was a family discussion but I can't recall if it was before or after you went out east). We are all trying not to blame Andrew, as he was Daddy's choice to manage the companies and it was Daddy's call to make, but it's difficult not to think that much of this is Andrew's fault.

Andrew says that he was lied to by investment bankers in New York, but the people we have looking into it say they didn't do anything to Andrew that they didn't do to anyone else. Andrew also appears to have been moving money around between different accounts to cover up some of the losses. I don't fully understand what he did but we all apparently signed off on it. I never read those documents so I'm as much to blame as anyone. We all probably should have been paying closer attention, especially since we all knew in our heart that Andrew wasn't up to the task.

The short of it is that the trust accounts are frozen, so we won't be getting our monthly allowance. I can't imagine this will be an immediate concern for you as you live so modestly, but it is going to be very difficult on Susie, who has to maintain that Rosedale monstrosity. And Bips has made a habit of spending all of it and more as he gets it. He's in London with no means of paying his hotel bill. Susie says he's got some sort of prescription-narcotic dependency.

I guess we thought we were part of the 1 percent, but it looks like we probably never did better than the top 2 or 3, ha ha.

I am glad that Daddy isn't around to see this. I think of him often.

Perhaps it won't be so painful for you. You always said the money held us back, so in a way this sets you free.

It is urgent that you call me, Natalie.

Martha

FIFTY-EIGHT

MATT CALLED THE Council meeting to order.

He was relieved to see that Alessandra was not in attendance. He had no idea what he would say to her. He had no idea what there was to say to her. "Alessandra, this is…"? What? What was it? He didn't know how to describe the situation in which they found themselves. He was racked with guilt over their tryst, felt it was horribly wrong. But could he say that he would not do it again?

Adoption of the agenda and the minutes of the last meeting. "Business arising?" said Matt.

Councillor Neary was on his feet. Another resolution to amend the development regulations so as to accommodate a development of the sort the original regulations were designed to prohibit. Maybe there was no point in bothering to regulate anything, thought Matt. That was a school of thought. Best-laid plans and all that. Maybe chaos was a force of nature and trying to stop anything a futile waste of energy that would merely, at best, delay the inevitable. Why should there be rules if not to check something that wanted, that was compelled by some fundamental law of the universe, to happen?

Matt looked up to the gallery. A few of the usual cranks in attendance, retirees with nothing better to do than fret about the bylaw concerning the keeping of laying hens or the naming of new streets. There were four reporters already near sleep. Jaysus, thought Matt, this really is the small-time.

Discretionary-use application for a hydroponic project to grow lettuces on Mullock Street and someone wanting to use their house on Cornwall Crescent as a yoga studio with the written approval of the neighbourhood. All on Council were in favour and said aye.

Planning Durnford was now answering a query about dramatic increases in the cost of providing water service to some new housing developments on the old Lucy land.

Matt checked his email.

From: katio6498@gmail.com
To: MOlford@st.john's.ca
Subject: wtf

Mom called to say she wanted me to move out of my apartment because it's inappropriate for an "unmarried woman" to be under the same roof as men? Is this for real? She was serious. I don't know how to respond. What is going on?

Indeed, thought Matt, what was going on.

Now Councillor Jardine was reporting on a public meeting he had attended on behalf of Council concerning the expansion of a high school in Cowan Heights. Planning Durnford was putting some drawings on an easel for Council to see. The proposed addition was breathtakingly ugly. But a school, thought Matt, soon to be neglected and covered in graffiti, what odds.

Alessandra entered. She made wide, hurried strides to her place, files clutched to her chest. Sunglasses up on her head. Her dress, coral-coloured and patterned with indigo stars such as a child might draw, was sleeveless, the scalloping of the neckline showing Matt places he'd so recently kissed. His cock stirred.

Alessandra looked to him and smiled. She gave him an ill-judged wave, thrice closing her fingers to her palm. Planning Durnford saw this and scowled. Matt remembered feeling Alessandra's heels digging into his ass. She'd said things in Italian he supposed she'd dare not say in English. Dear God, he thought. Alessandra glanced at the drawing on the easel and made a face showing her disgust for the new school's design.

Proposal for the expansion of the dog park at Mundy Pond. Dog-lover Wally O'Neill speaking in favour and a vote. Passed unanimously.

Councillor Shea was on about storm sewers. Storm sewers were a municipal issue; if Matt were in Ottawa he would not be hearing about storm sewers. Ottawa was an opportunity but it was also a sanctuary.

Councillor Wendy Kennedy, looking solemn, expressing the City's sadness over the death of Royal Newfoundland Constabulary Inspector Gary Mackenzie in the line of duty. She has drafted a letter. Planning Durnford saying something.

Matt heard that the policeman was likely knocked down by a truck he pulled over, a vehicular assault. Before the meeting Planning Durnford had taken Matt aside to share what he knew. Heavy rain that day meant the investigators couldn't get a conclusive tire track from the scene. They somehow gleaned it was a pickup and suspected that Mackenzie had unwittingly pulled over a vehicle with drugs aboard or with a driver on an outstanding warrant. There was a new class of villain in town, feasting on the boom-town bucks. The cops knew who they were and linked them to Mackenzie's death. Why Planning Durnford should be in the loop Matt did not know. Durnford was a card-carrying Conservative and they were thick with the Constabulary. Was it bullshit? Did Durnford know Matt had been recruited to run for his team? That would so piss Durnford off. Unless Durnford was in on it. Could that be?

Councillor Neary was on his feet. Matt glanced at the agenda on his tablet. He thought they were done.

"The deer problem in Bowring Park," Neary said. "Could I move that it be added to the agenda?"

"Rather more a matter for the private meeting, don't you think, Councillor Neary?" said Matt. "The unfortunate gentleman's privacy is an issue, is it not?"

"We're past that," volunteered Councillor Mercer.

"Indeed," said Planning Durnford from his seat.

"It's public. It is," said Councillor Kennedy.

"There are those who would argue that the idea of privacy is outmoded," said Alessandra, though to whom Matt could not guess.

"I thought the police had taken care of the matter," said Matt, "but I had heard he was back."

"He was detained and held for a psychiatric examination," said Planning Durnford, standing. "Obviously he was released and has returned to the park. The situation has to be dealt with, Your Worship. We have tourists going up there to see if they can get a look, and Miss Devereaux, who is the acting director at Parks, has been getting some truly bizarre mail."

"Catch and release," said Councillor Jardine.

"He's got a lot of support in the community," offered Councillor Mercer.

"Says who?" asked Neary.

"Faccbook, I s'pose," said Mercer.

"This is one of those stories that'll . . . whaddaya call it? Go viral."

"Deer has ticks, right?" Wally asked no one in particular. "Deer ticks."

"Deer aren't native to Newfoundland," said Jardine.

"We talked to some of the supporters," said Alessandra.

"Whasit called? Lymes disease?" said Wally.

"Who 'talked to some of the supporters'?" asked Councillor Jardine.

"They came to see the mayor and myself after a meeting of the Parks and Public Spaces Committee," said Alessandra.

"I'm on Parks and Public Spaces. First I've heard of this," said Councillor Neary.

"You were absent from the meeting, Councillor Neary," said Alessandra, "and not for the first time."

"I considered it a trivial matter at the time and I'm still not sure it isn't," said Matt. Neary's hand was up. "Order everyone. Councillor Neary has the floor."

"Thank you, Your Worship. I want to go on the record in saying that not everybody supports this deer man. I have been contacted by some of my Ward 3 constituents who are very concerned about the example this sets for youth, especially those very young children who might like pretending they are some sort of animal."

"The park is in Ward 5, Councillor Neary, my ward," said Wally.

"I appreciate that, Councillor O'Neill," said Neary. "That's not the issue. It's that parents are concerned that their kids might see the lifestyle as an option."

"What are our options?" asked Jardine.

"Can we not get a peace bond?" Matt was losing patience.

"Better be careful," said Wally. "People are going to say it's hes' right to be whatever he wants to be. He could have been born dat way." Wally did a chair-bound dance, his raised hands open and flat, his shoulders pumping to a beat in his head.

"A doe?" asked Neary. "Or is it a buck?"

"Doe a deer, a female deer," sang Jardine.

"No, a fawn," said Councillor Kennedy. "You are born a fawn."

"I was born a buck bayman," said Wally.

"Buddy could always get a job as a service animal, I suppose," said Jardine. "No one has any problem with a Seeing Eye dog doing whatever it likes. Who complains about shit from a police horse?"

"Can we all agree," said Matt, "that we have no quarrel with the man's wish to act like a deer?"

"To *be* a deer—that's really important to the supporters," said Mercer.

"Diversity, right, we supports diversity," said Councillor Dunn. "Takes all kinds, right?"

"And biodiversity." Councillor Jardine was almost cackling. "That's a plus. This is like, diversity and biodiversity. We have a man who is a deer resident in the urban forest. Eleven out of ten. Spark up the sweetgrass."

"I cannot believe you said that, Councillor Jardine." Councillor Kennedy was, as Matt had never before seen her, in a lather. "There is nothing to joke about! Mockery serves no purpose. You think it puts you above things but it's merely your way of avoiding responsibility! This is about accepting people for who they are!"

"But he's not a 'person,' is he?" Jardine's humour, good or ill, had left him. He was barking at Kennedy.

"Order, please. Order," said Matt. "Okay. Let's say the City of St. John's is willing to go so far as to acknowledge Mr. Davenant *is* a deer. Can we move on from there and say the deer is trespassing?"

"Can an animal be charged with an offence?" asked Jardine.

"In the old days a problem animal would be destroyed. Now they're much more likely to be relocated," said Neary.

"Tranquilizer dart, right in the arse," said Wally.

"Call him an invasive species," said Jardine. "Then he's the feds' problem."

"In Invermere, British Columbia," said Planning Durnford,

"deer overpopulation is a serious issue. They carry disease, are a hindrance to traffic, and when they proposed a cull they were met with a lot of opposition."

"Christ sakes," Matt let slip, turning staff heads and stirring the gallery. He looked up and saw that the men and women of the press were scribbling furiously. They were fewer in number and younger all the time and gasping for content to fill ever more platforms. They were loving this. Bow-tied bastard from the *Telegram* had a shit-eating grin. Missus from CBC looked to be giggling.

"Maybe he's one of those animal rights extremists," said Jardine, "in deep cover."

"See, you got to be careful," said Wally. "Human rights is one t'ing, but if the foolishness surrounding the seal hunt has shown us anyt'ing it's dat the animal rights trumps human rights every time. Animal rights is nuclear."

"Wally, you are so stupid," Alessandra said.

You couldn't say "stupid" anymore.

Matt saw Wally flinch, like he'd been stung. Mercer and Neary and Jardine and Kennedy were all looking to one another, confirming they'd heard right. One was no longer allowed to call someone stupid.

"I think," said Matt, "what Councillor Cappello meant to say is that we needn't be concerned about the animal rights movement in this case."

"Can dey tag-team like dat?" Wally, for some reason, was putting his question to Planning Durnford, like it was a procedural matter. "It's a conflict of interest or something, isn't it? You know, the mayor and Councillor Cappello ganging up on me where de'er an item deese days?"

The chamber went quiet. Matt could hear the whirring of a computer drive, the building's air exchange system, a sneeze down the corridor outside. He knew he needed to fill the silence fast but found himself struggling to find words.

"Deer? What do you mean 'deer an item'?" Councillor Cappello was confused.

"'They are,'" translated Councillor Kennedy. "'Where *they* are an item these days.'"

Matt opened his mouth to speak but it seemed the air was rushing in to gag him. Alessandra shrugged theatrically.

"What's that got to do with anything?" she said.

MATT COULDN'T REMEMBER much of the rest of the Council meeting. He looked to Alessandra and she met his eye but he could not intuit what she was thinking.

Jardine sensed that Matt was staggered, was stunned, was skating to the bench concussed and had the decency to move that discussion concerning Harry Davenant, thespian, security guard, deer/man of Bowring Park, be tabled.

Jardine then promptly moved they adjourn.

FIFTY-NINE

ALESSANDRA SAW THE reporter from the *Telegram* standing by her car, an ambush. Matt's Camry was already gone from its reserved space. He must have sprinted from the meeting and sped away to avoid just the sort of mortifying interrogation she was about to face. Was Matt cannier than she or merely a coward?

She supposed the reporter was going to ask her why she had, not ten minutes earlier, so freely and publicly admitted that she and the mayor were, in the words of Wally O'Neill, "an item."

More humiliating than the revelation was the fact it wasn't true. She and Matt spent an afternoon together and there would never be another. Alessandra saw now that she'd let herself imagine there was more to the assignation than there was. It was not love she had mistaken; she'd never dreamed of love. But she had let herself imagine companionship and intimacy. She'd let herself picture the two of them on a weekend trip to

New York or Montreal, walking about, having a meal, going
to the galleries, fucking with abandon when they got back to
the hotel, breakfast in bed with the papers. How silly she was.
Matt's regret over their tryst was nearly remorse; it was written
on his face when they'd driven back from the motel.

She liked this fellow from the *Telegram* but she decided she
had no intention of discussing what had just transpired in the
Council chamber. Prying into that wasn't journalism; it was
prurience.

"Ms. Cappello?"

"Yes, yes," she said, her hand reaching for her car door.

"Could you answer a few questions about Kavanagh Court?"

Alessandra stopped and turned to the young man. He was
in a cheap suit, the sort Matt could get away with as this kid
could not. He wore an older man's bow tie. He couldn't look
her in the eye, embarrassed, perhaps, by the situation of this
middle-aged minx.

"Sure," she said.

"What's going on there? I've got contradictory information.
There is going to be a park built, but you were against that?
And the corporate sponsorship is a problem for you? Is that
correct?" he asked.

"No. I was against some cookie-cutter park, something
out of a box. And the sponsorship was conditional on a lot of
unnecessary signage and interpretation that will essentially
be advertising."

"But Jerjuice was going to pay for the costs of developing
the park?"

"Yes."

"Okay, so you were proposing what instead?" He held a notepad but wasn't writing anything down.

"Letting it take its own shape," she answered. "Maybe leaving it be."

"Okay."

"Clear?"

"That's never going to happen," he said. "Leaving it be."

"Probably not. They are going to let it break in order to discover what went wrong."

Alessandra opened the door to her car and climbed in.

ALESSANDRA CALLED OUT to Jules as she entered the house but it was not enough to wake him. She found him sound asleep in his window-lit chair in the living room, a book in his lap. Drowsiness was a potential side effect of the Reminyl. She didn't mind admitting to herself she was as happy to find him this way as awake.

She went to his side.

His breathing was slow and steady. He was far away. Did his dreams fragment along with his mind, she wondered. Did there remain tiny islands of lucidity in his unconscious? Could his waking life now be more dreamlike, more nightmarish than sleep?

Jules himself was the author of the volume fanned on his lap. *Bristol Intelligence: Aural Accounts of a New-World Fishery and the First Chabotto Voyage.* Alessandra had never before seen him return to one of his own books. Was he looking there for knowledge he'd acquired and lost, or for evidence of the person he knew he once was? Did he now pore over his own words with bafflement or with nostalgia? What happened when the reader no longer recognized himself as the author?

There'd been a great stir in Cabot studies some years earlier when a fellow expert in the field, Alwyn Ruddock, had her papers, including what were rumoured to be significant new primary documents, destroyed upon her death.

No one would ever know whether her claims of pending revelations were a lie to prop up her reputation or genuine discoveries that, because of a sense of ownership or professional jealousy, she could not bear to see in the hands of peers who outlived her.

Ruddock said before dying that she was in possession of evidence that Cabot was not lost at sea on a second journey across the Atlantic, as had long been the understanding, but that he returned to London in 1500 after an epic voyage to the New World.

That was a happier ending to the story, wasn't it, safe return rather than consignment to the deeps?

And was there not a third alternative, one so chilling it could scarcely be considered? That Cabot and his men were stranded in Newfoundland. That they had crippled to some rocky shore in boats so damaged, hulls punctured by ice, sails flayed, that they could not take them back the way they came. That they survived the crossing but would never go home and never be found.

Alessandra realized that if Jules forgot her he would not miss her when she was gone.

SIXTY

MATT DIDN'T STICK around City Hall when the meeting concluded. Before the press could pack up their notebooks and
laptops and come downstairs to confront him he was already
in his Camry.

He knew he was driving out to Bowring Park but was
unsure why.

There wasn't an hour of daylight left.

It was a sultry evening so Matt motored with the windows
down. He could smell barbecuing meat and cut grass. Hot
nights such as these were rare in St. John's, so the livyers appre-
ciated them that much more. There was an air of celebration
in the town. The people Matt saw on the streets, in their shorts
and tank tops and sandals, looked so happy. Happy!

He parked the Camry at the park's maintenance depot, near
the western service entrance, and went on foot.

A man was a deer.

There were certain things dealt you; you were in many,

many ways, simply what you were.

Which was what? What were the qualities of being human? Deer weren't self-aware, so one couldn't consciously live as one. Did the trees have some essential quality of being trees or were qualities merely something observed or assigned by man?

He passed close by a soccer pitch. The players were young boys, around nine or ten years old, their high calls a musical ornament over the soprano and alto, tenor and bass encouragements of their parents on the sidelines. Matt loved the sound of children's voices and missed those of his own.

This Harry Davenant character, when had he ever stated he was a deer? Surely deer didn't proclaim. Was there a final moment of humanity where he signed off, said, "This is the last you will hear from me as I will be taking the deer's silent ways."

No, someone asserted he was a deer and for some reason people supported the proposition. Davenant was nominated and elected deer. The people wanted a deer.

Matt took a foot trail into the woods, a path off the course prescribed by those who set the rules on this patch of the world. What had Alessandra said? Parks were like zoos? This is what she would have for her preserve, not the broad flat courses of crushed stone, but narrow cuts in the ground, rabbit runs found and worn wide as a man's way. But we weren't wild things. We were broken and trained. Perhaps Harry Davenant had only jumped his paddock fence and lit out for the open country.

What was that scent that rose from the forest floor, that delectable aroma that was at once decay and bloom, carrion and fallen fruit?

Matt stopped and looked. The trees were close around him. There was no heat from the sun and that which accumulated in the ground through the day was dissipating. No one could see him here.

Why had Alessandra confessed their tryst? It wasn't a mistake of a second tongue; she was far too smart, perfectly fluent. She bore Matt no malice; it wasn't vengeful. It was likely nothing to do with Matt at all. "What does *that* have to do with anything?" "That," she said. "That" was a thing; "that" was a fact she wasn't going to waste any effort denying.

Why was he here? Why had he come to Bowring Park? Was he looking for Harry Davenant? No. Maybe. He kept on, getting deep enough into the woods that, besides the birds and insects, the only sound he could hear was of the traffic humming on the arterial road on the south side. How far would one have to walk into the forest, he wondered, before you'd stop hearing man's echo, the ghosting of his incessant noise? There were always planes overhead so maybe it was no longer possible.

On the path before him was the carcass of a crow, its body bug-eaten and in advanced decomposition but its wings still glossy and full. Of what were feathers composed that they resisted decay?

Harry Davenant was an actor, a showman. Matt and he shared that. They'd heard the cheering and the jeering from the stands. They knew the crowd and its moods.

His knee was singing. In the game they said, "Play through pain" and for the first time, Matt, thinking about it, understood the phrase had more than one meaning. What portion of life was misunderstood? How many actions were inspired by the equivalent of the misheard lyrics of a popular song? There was wisdom in seeing things as they were but was there not an even greater insight in knowing things as they were not? In recognizing that a commonly held truth was fundamentally in error, or what was long thought wrong was right? He wasn't thinking straight.

In sport you learned there was no future. There was a past, a record, a matrix of statistics that marked your trail. There was the electric present. But there was no future. The proof was in the futility of game plans. No matter the challenge it was always faced with a study of the opponents' perceived strengths and weaknesses, strategies offensive and defensive, tactics and set plays. All of which ceased to be of any relevance the moment the puck dropped and the exquisite and terrifying unpredictability of the next moment exploded from the now and you responded with instinct, with lunging and clawing. Everything was accident and yet, next match, you planned again. Planning was as futile as prayer.

Matt could hear the river below. He was skirting the crevasse but could not see the edge through the green growth of summer.

What would he do with himself now? He fancied he might go back to school. Be one of those "mature students." Why not? His undergraduate degree was a hockey scholarship joke, but now, years late, he was thinking back on much of what he missed with curiosity. "In the long run we are all dead" was the case for the present, for paying heed to the here and now, sad and funny at once.

The best you could do was to acknowledge things and get on with it. Dream as one might of flight on waking, it was walking the miles that got you there. Man was not winged. Man was not hooved or horned. Man was trapped in man's body.

He kept on, his course tracing that of the river below.

ACKNOWLEDGMENTS

Steve Crocker helped me address the question of the animal. Steve Palmer proofed Spanish invention, Christina Fabretto Italian, and Claire Wilkshire French. Dr. Jasber Gill consulted on psychiatry, Jamie Fitzpatrick on hockey.

I regularly discussed the novel's progress with Charlie Tomlinson as we walked our dogs and benefited from his sage advice.

Fans of *The Great Eastern* will recognize Bill Murphy's trick, the Skin wetlands and the fierce Tuskaweegee.

Gerry Porter and Debbie McGee eagle-eyed the manuscript and showed me the error of my ways.

I am grateful for the support of The Newfoundland and Labrador Arts Council, The City of St. John's and Memorial University of Newfoundland 's Writer In Residence program.

Among the many heroes at House of Anansi, I especially want to thank Sarah MacLachlan and Janice Zawerbny.

EDWARD RICHE, an award-winning writer for page, stage, and screen, was born in Botwood on the Bay of Exploits on the northeast coast of Newfoundland. His first novel, *Rare Birds*, was adapted into a major motion picture starring William Hurt and Molly Parker, and his second novel, *The Nine Planets*, was a *Globe and Mail* Best Book and won the Thomas Raddall Head Award. He is also the author of *Easy to Like*, which was a finalist for the Winterset Award and longlisted for the International IMPAC Dublin Literary Award. Riche lives in St. John's, Newfoundland.